“Our parents are appleheads!”

An icy shiver went up Katie’s spine as her eyes locked on the doll with the bright green eyes.

“Andy . . .” Katie managed to squeak, pointing to the top shelf.

Andy looked up. His face went pale. “It’s Mom and Dad!” he gasped. “Isn’t it?”

For a moment Katie couldn’t speak. She’d never seen anything so horrifying. Her mother’s beautiful face was squished up and rotting. Her dad’s funny grin was carved into a twisted sneer.

“Our parents are appleheads!” she shrieked.

Starscape Books by Annette Cascone and Gina Cascone

Deadtime Stories®

Grave Secrets

The Witching Game

The Beast of Baskerville

Invasion of the Appleheads

Little Magic Shop of Horrors

Grandpa's Monster Movies

INVASION OF THE APPLEHEADS

Deadtime Stories logo by Bill Villareal

A Starscape Book
Published by Tom Doherty Associates, LLC
175 Fifth Avenue
New York, NY 10010

www.tor-forge.com

The Library of Congress has cataloged the hardcover edition as follows:

Cascone, Annette.
Invasion of the Appleheads / Annette Cascone and Gina Cascone.—1st ed.
p. cm.
"A Tom Doherty Associates book."
ISBN 978-0-7653-3068-0 (hardcover)
ISBN 978-1-4299-9295-4 (e-book)
1. Zombies—Fiction. 2. Horror stories. I. Cascone, Gina. II. Title.
PZ7.C26673 In 2012
[Fic]—dc22

2012011655

ISBN 978-0-7653-3074-1 (trade paperback)

Starscape books may be purchased for educational, business, or promotional use. For information on bulk purchases, please contact Macmillan Corporate and Premium Sales Department at 1-800-221-7945, extension 5442, or write specialmarkets@macmillan.com.

First Edition: July 2012
First Trade Paperback Edition: January 2014

Printed in the United States of America

0 9 8 7 6 5 4 3 2 1

INVASION OF THE APPLEHEADS

ANNETTE CASCONE and GINA CASCONE

A TOM DOHERTY ASSOCIATES BOOK • NEW YORK

For Roger Williams,

for working tirelessly to move us forward—

as authors, as clients, as sisters, and, occasionally,

as a couple of appleheads

INVASION OF THE APPLEHEADS

1

Katie Lawrence was sure the torture would never end. She had to struggle to hold back the scream in her throat. Because she knew that if she screamed, things would only get worse.

That is, if things *could* get worse.

"Isn't this fun, kids?" Katie's mother asked cheerily.

No! Katie wanted to yell at the top of her lungs. *This is not fun! This is the worst possible way to spend a day!*

It was a beautiful, sunny Sunday. It was also the day before Halloween. That's what made things really bad.

Katie wanted to be home putting the finishing

touches on her Halloween costume and getting ready for the big parade. The Halloween parade was the biggest event in Appleton. All of the kids in Katie's school were excited about it.

Katie was excited about it, too, especially since she'd been invited to a party by Christine Baker, the most popular girl in her class. Starting the fifth grade in a new school had been hard enough, but making new friends had been even harder.

Unfortunately, Katie wasn't at home right now working on her Halloween costume. Because Katie was crammed into the backseat of the car with her eleven-year-old brother, Andy, who didn't want to be driving around Appleton any more than she did. All because their parents had insisted they spend the day together visiting the town's historical sights.

"Are we going to stop soon?" Andy moaned.

"Yes," Mrs. Lawrence answered. "We're almost there."

"Almost where?" Katie whispered to her brother. "What stupid thing are we going to have to look at next?"

"Probably the biggest rock in Appleton," Andy whispered back.

They both snickered.

Katie and her family had moved to Appleton just a few months before. They used to live in the city, but Katie's parents had decided that a small town would be a much better place for them to grow up.

Appleton *was* a small town. It was a small *creepy* town, in Katie's opinion. It had been founded in the 1600s, and most of it still looked four hundred years old. Even the neighborhood Katie and her family lived in looked like a page from a history book.

Traveling through Appleton was like driving through a time warp. Except for the mall, there was nothing modern-looking at all.

Katie hated it.

But her parents adored it. They thought Appleton was the greatest place in the universe.

The morning before, Katie's mother had picked up a little guidebook at the library that told about all the historical sights in their new town. Before the day was over, they were going to visit every single one of them.

"I can't believe we spent twenty minutes looking at a stupid piece of cement," Katie complained to Andy.

Even though Katie had whispered, her mother heard her. "What piece of cement?" she asked.

"The one that said 'George Washington crossed here,'" Katie answered. "What was so interesting about that?"

"That was very interesting," Mr. Lawrence answered. "It was the route that Washington took on his way to an important battle of the Revolution," he started to explain. "He—"

"I know. I know." Katie stopped her father. She couldn't stand to hear the story again. History was just about her least favorite subject in the world.

"So what are we going to see next?" Andy asked, sounding as impatient as Katie felt.

"The next stop is the Appleton Orchard," Mrs. Lawrence said, checking the guidebook.

Katie and Andy rolled their eyes.

"Do you want to hear what the guidebook says about it?" their mother asked.

"Noooooo!" Katie and Andy answered at the same time.

"Of course we do," Mr. Lawrence said, shooting Katie and Andy a scolding look over his shoulder.

"I think you kids are really going to like this," their mother told them.

She'd been promising that all day. It hadn't been true yet.

" 'The Appleton Orchard was originally owned by a woman who was accused of being a witch,' " Mrs. Lawrence read.

"Sounds pretty spooky, kids," Mr. Lawrence chimed in, trying to stir up their interest.

"Listen to this." Their mother continued to read. " 'The townspeople believed that the witch was putting some kind of magic potion into her apples, a potion that turned all the children of Appleton into zombies. On Halloween Night, three hundred years ago, the angry parents burned the orchard to the ground.' "

"Pretty cool!" Andy said.

Katie agreed the story was cool, but she still wasn't sure about going there. "If the orchard was burned to the ground, what is there to see?" she pointed out.

"The book says that the witch's house is still standing," her mother told her. "It's the oldest house in Appleton. And it wasn't even damaged in the fire."

Who wanted to see another stupid old house? Katie slumped against the car door. Things *had* gotten worse.

"Look at that," Mr. Lawrence said a second later as the orchard came into view.

A banner stretched across the road. It read WELCOME TO APPLETON ORCHARD.

There were hand-painted signs posted every few feet. *Free Candy Apples! Free Apple Cider! Free Haunted Hayrides!*

"I thought this place was supposed to be deserted," Katie said.

"Well, it certainly looks full of life today," her father replied as he drove toward the huge iron gates that led into the orchard. "Maybe someone has taken over the place. This looks like some kind of grand-opening celebration."

"That's funny," Mrs. Lawrence chimed in. "I didn't see anything about it in the paper this morning. If I had, we could have skipped the sightseeing tour and spent the day here."

Katie shot her brother a look. Too bad there hadn't been anything in the paper. The orchard sounded a *little* more interesting than anything else they'd seen so far. Maybe they could have been spared a whole day of torture.

"Well, we're here now," Mr. Lawrence said, turning through the gates. "And we've still got a couple of good hours before it gets dark."

As they entered the grounds, Katie felt something strange. Something that made her shiver. It was as if she'd passed through some kind of invisible wall, or like diving into a pool and breaking through the surface of the water. And it happened just as quickly.

Strangely, outside the gates, the trees were turning colors and losing their leaves, but inside the gates, the apple trees were at their prime—green and loaded with fruit.

Katie turned around in her seat to look back at the gates.

Something else was wrong. But it took Katie a minute to figure out what it was.

Outside the gates, where the leaves on the trees were dying, it was a beautiful, sunny day. But inside the gates, where everything flourished, it was dark and dreary.

Katie shivered again. "Creepy," she said, talking to herself.

"What's creepy?" her mother asked.

"The trees," Katie answered. "How come they've still got apples?"

"Maybe the apple season is longer out here in the country," her mother said.

"But look how dark it is in here," Katie pointed out.

Her father laughed. "Of course it's dark," he said. "We're in the shadow of all these trees."

Katie caught a glimpse of the sky above the trees. It was steely gray, with no sunshine at all.

But before Katie could point that out to her family, the words stuck in her throat as a hideous creature stepped out from between the apple trees that lined the drive. Its head was swollen, and the green, putrid skin that covered its face was rotting right off its skull. Bloodshot eyeballs hung from their sockets. And a blood-covered ax stuck out of its chest.

"Look!" Mrs. Lawrence exclaimed as another grotesque creature appeared ahead of them. "Everyone is dressed up for Halloween!"

Katie took a good look at the creature with the ax in its chest. If that was a costume, it was very, very good.

"This is excellent!" Andy said. "I definitely want to go on the haunted hayride."

"Didn't I tell you this would be fun?" Mrs. Lawrence said.

They pulled into the parking lot under a giant old shade tree where several other cars were already parked. But there were no other people in the parking lot, just the biggest, creepiest-looking scarecrow on a pole that Katie had ever seen.

Its head was the size of a basketball, and it was covered with a dirty white sheet that was tied around its neck with a thick, heavy rope dangling to the ground like a leash. Its face was painted onto the sheet.

The second her father parked the car, the creature started to move!

Katie let out a loud, startled cry.

So did her mother.

"It's all right," Katie's father assured them. "It's just someone dressed up in a Halloween costume."

The giant creature climbed down from its pole and started clomping its way toward them, flailing its arms and moaning. It looked like Frankenstein's monster dressed up as a scarecrow.

No one made a move to get out of the car.

"If he's trying to scare us away, he's doing a pretty good job," Katie's mother said nervously.

The scarecrow fell onto the hood of the car, moaning and groaning even louder than before.

"Let's get out of here!" Katie cried.

But it was too late.

Within seconds, the car was surrounded by cackling witches and blood-covered ghouls.

And Katie had the horrible feeling that they weren't just people in Halloween costumes.

2

"OOOOOOOO-WAAAAAAAY!" the scarecrow moaned, peering through the windshield at them. "OOOOOOOO-WAAAAAAAAY!"

Katie could see the scarecrow's beady black eyes glaring at them from behind the sheet with his painted-on face. His body was so huge and bulky, it covered the entire hood of the car.

Katie's heart pounded against her chest even harder than the scarecrow's massive fists were pounding the glass.

"Do something, Dad!" Katie yelled.

"Everybody just stay calm," Mr. Lawrence said, sounding anything *but* calm. "I'm sure he's just acting scary for Halloween."

"Then he's a really good actor!" Katie shot back. "Cause he's scaring me half to death!"

"*OOOOOOOOOOO-WAAAAAAAAY!*" the scarecrow kept moaning.

"What in the world is he saying?" Mrs. Lawrence said. She sounded pretty scared herself.

"I don't know," Mr. Lawrence answered, shooting Mrs. Lawrence a worried look.

Katie didn't want to know. She just wanted to get out of there. Fast!

"Back up, Dad!" Katie cried.

"He can't back up!" Andy said. "He'll run over all those ghouls on our trunk!"

The ghouls weren't just climbing on the trunk. They were banging on the windows and hanging off the roof.

Just then another voice screeched through the air.

"*OOOOOOOO-WEN!*" the voice bellowed. "Get

away from that car before I turn you into a tongueless little rat! All of you! Away from the car!"

The wrinkled old woman who raced toward the car looked even more horrible than she sounded. She was dressed in a witch's costume.

But Katie didn't think she had on any makeup at all. Her shriveled old skin really was a sickly green color. And the hairy wart hanging from the end of her nose wasn't glued on.

"Oh, look." Mrs. Lawrence relaxed as the witch swatted the ghouls with her broom. "They're just putting on a little show for us," she said.

"Get away from the car, Owen," the gnarled old woman growled. Then she grabbed the rope hanging from the scarecrow's neck and gave it a tug. "Keep it up, and I'll lock you back in the dungeon!"

The scarecrow quickly climbed down from the hood. He was shaking and cowering. Katie had the feeling he really was afraid of the witch.

"Bad Owen," the witch hollered, waving her gnarled finger in front of his face. "Bad, bad Owen."

"Owen?" Andy rolled his eyes. "The scarecrow's name is Owen?"

"He looks more like Frankenstein to me," Katie said.

Mrs. Lawrence laughed. "You see?" she said. "Everything is fine!"

"Welcome to Appleton Orchard!" The witch cackled as she pressed her hairy wart nose up against Katie's window. "Come out, dear," she said, beckoning Katie with a crooked finger. Then she reached into her pocket and pulled out a huge clump of peanut brittle. "I have lots of goodies for you!"

3

Katie shot her parents a look that said, *Please don't make me get out of this car!* But her parents were already climbing out themselves.

"Don't be afraid," the witch said as she pulled open Katie's door. "We're just having fun. Aren't we, Owen?"

The scarecrow let out a nervous moan as the witch bit off a piece of the peanut brittle she held in her twisted fingers.

Katie drew back at the sight of the gooey brown gunk swishing around the witch's stained yellow teeth.

"That's one heck of a welcoming committee you've

got there," Mr. Lawrence said as he headed toward the witch.

"It sure is," Mrs. Lawrence agreed. "For a second, you even had *us* fooled."

"I hope we didn't scare you too badly," the witch said. "Our scarecrow loves Halloween. And he loves trying to scare all the children away. Don't you, Owen?" she growled.

Owen didn't answer. He just lowered his head as if he were ashamed.

"Don't mind him," the witch said. She winked at Andy. "The cat bit off Owen's tongue when he was just a little boy. And she swallowed it right up!"

Katie and Andy exchanged nervous glances as the witch started to cackle.

"I'm Yaga," she said, sticking out her hand to Katie. "And you're my next victim."

Yaga had the worst breath Katie had ever smelled. It was so foul, Katie wanted to cover her nose. Only she wasn't about to touch her face. Not after shaking Yaga's hand. The witch's palm was as slimy as an eel.

"So, how long have you been here, Yaga?" Mrs. Lawrence asked.

"Hundreds of years," Yaga answered, biting off another piece of peanut brittle.

Katie's mother laughed. "I mean, how long has the orchard been open?"

"Today," Yaga answered. "It's our grand opening. That's why everything is free."

"That's what we thought," Mrs. Lawrence told her. "But we didn't see any announcement in the paper this morning."

Yaga chuckled. "We don't like to advertise," she said. "We have plenty of *other* ways to get customers."

Just then another old witch headed toward them, carrying a tray loaded with candy apples and steaming hot cups.

"Can Drusila and I offer you some hot apple cider and sweet candy apples before you set off on the scariest hayride of your lives?" Yaga asked.

"I'd love some hot apple cider," Mrs. Lawrence said.

"Me, too," added Mr. Lawrence.

"I brewed it myself," Yaga said, handing over the cups. "It does wonders for your head."

Mrs. Lawrence looked at Yaga, confused.

Yaga's lips twisted into a ghoulish grin. "It clears the sinuses," she said.

"Oh." Mrs. Lawrence nodded politely, then took a sip. "Mmmm . . . it's absolutely delicious."

"How about some candy apples for you two?" Drusila, the other witch, asked Katie and Andy. She smiled, exposing her four rotten teeth.

"I'd like one," Andy said, reaching for an apple.

"And you, my little pretty?" Drusila leered at Katie.

"Sure," Katie said, taking one. "Thanks."

Drusila kept right on leering. "You have beautiful eyes," she told Katie. "Look how green and full of life they are!" Drusila seemed so excited by Katie's eyes that she was actually snorting with glee.

"They *are* full of life, aren't they?" Yaga grinned, leering at Katie, too.

Yaga's stare sent shivers racing across Katie's flesh.

Yaga's eyes were the creepiest part of her. The left one was grayer than charcoal, but the right one was so blue and sparkling, it looked like crystal. Katie couldn't turn away from her hypnotic stare.

It was as if Yaga's eyes were trying to suck the life right out of her.

"Katie has her mother's eyes," Mr. Lawrence said, pulling Yaga's attention away from Katie.

"She does at that," Yaga agreed, peering at Mrs. Lawrence. "Your eyes are as green as emeralds, too. They're enticing," she told Mrs. Lawrence.

"Thank you," Mrs. Lawrence acknowledged the compliment. Then she glanced at the house that stood at the far side of the parking lot. "After the hayride, I'd love to go inside the house. I understand it's the oldest house in Appleton."

Katie looked at the rickety old building. The huge gray stone walls were cracking and crumbling, and the wooden steps that led up to the door were rotting away. Thick, heavy grime covered the windows, and the shutters were hanging half off. Katie couldn't understand why in the world her mother would want to go in there. It didn't even look safe.

"Yes." Yaga smiled her ugly smile. "Of course you'll see the house. Our little gift shop is inside. That's where everyone ends up. But first, you must go on the hayride." Yaga clapped her hands loudly. "Owen!" she bellowed. "Prepare the next cart!"

"Oh, no," Andy whispered to Katie. "Not Owen."

Katie didn't want to get in a cart with Owen, either. But it didn't look like they had a choice. In the far distance, Katie now saw that the only other cart was already loaded with another set of parents and their two kids. Katie had never seen so much red hair in her life. It looked like a carriage full of rooster heads.

"Just go on over to the barn," Yaga said. "Owen will take real good care of you folks."

"Thanks, Yaga," Mr. Lawrence said. "I haven't been on a hayride in years. This is going to be great!"

Mrs. Lawrence giggled. "A *haunted* hayride," she reminded Mr. Lawrence. "Good thing you'll be with me," she added, taking his hand. "In case I get scared."

"I'll be listening for your screams." Yaga laughed.

Mr. and Mrs. Lawrence grinned as they raced for the barn.

Katie couldn't believe how goofy her parents were acting. It was almost like *they* were the kids and she and Andy were the adults.

"*OOOO-BAAACK*," Owen grunted as they reached the cart.

"Okay," Mr. Lawrence agreed. "I'll go in the back." He climbed up into the cart.

Mrs. Lawrence got in next.

"*Oooo-baaaack*," Mr. Lawrence said, imitating Owen with a chuckle. "That's such a great monster voice."

Mrs. Lawrence giggled again as she sat down next to her husband.

Owen just moaned.

Andy climbed in next and sat opposite his parents. Katie plunked herself down alongside Andy as Owen turned around and settled into the driver's seat. Then he snapped the reins hard, and the horses started to pull the cart forward.

"Here we go!" Mrs. Lawrence exclaimed.

"Isn't this neat?" Mr. Lawrence said, taking a sip of his cider.

The cart headed down the dusty old path toward the twisted apple trees. There were so many trees up ahead, it looked more like a forest than an orchard.

Katie unwrapped the candy apple Drusila had given her as she settled in for the ride. So far the orchard had been more interesting than she'd expected, but she still wanted to go home to prepare for Halloween. With any luck, the ride would be over by the time she finished her apple.

Katie lifted the apple to her mouth and bit off a huge, juicy chunk. The second the apple hit Katie's tongue, the sugary-sweet taste dissolved into something bitter and foul—and sickeningly slimy.

Katie's stomach rose up to her throat. The chunk of gunk in her mouth was moving! Katie could feel something squiggling across her tongue!

4

"A worm!" Katie spit out the piece of apple in her mouth. "There's a worm in my candy apple!" she shrieked.

"Let me see," Andy said.

Katie kept right on spitting as she shoved her candy apple under Andy's nose.

Sure enough, there was a rotten brown spot right where she'd bitten into the apple. In the center was a little hole where half a worm was squiggling around.

"Gross!" Andy said, pushing Katie's apple away from his face.

"Yuck! Yuck! Yuck!" Katie hurled the apple over the

side of the cart as hard as she could. Then she grabbed a handful of tissues from her jacket pocket and started wiping her tongue with them. She'd never be able to get the taste of worm out of her mouth.

"Calm down, Katie," her mother said. "I know it's awful to find a worm in your apple. But it's not going to kill you. Forget about it."

Easy for her to say! Katie thought. *She isn't the one who bit into a worm!*

Andy nodded. Then he pitched his candy apple out of the cart, too. "Some haunted hayride," he said. "So far all we've gotten is rotten candy apples."

"For real," Katie agreed. "It was scarier in the parking lot."

As the cart moved ahead, Katie could see a bunch of kids out in the orchards picking apples. Some of them went to her school.

"Mark," Katie called out to one of the boys she recognized. He was up on a ladder picking apples from a tree.

Only he didn't answer.

"Hey, Mark," she called out again, a little bit louder this time. "What are you doing here?"

He still didn't answer. He didn't even look her way. He just kept picking apples, moving his arms up and down like a robot.

"Mark!" she shouted as the cart passed right by him.

Nothing.

"Who's that?" Andy teased her. "Your boyfriend?"

"No," Katie answered. "He's just a kid from school."

"He seems like a real jerk," Andy said.

"He's not a jerk," Katie said. Actually, Mark was one of the nicest kids in her class. He had even shown her around on the first day of school. Katie couldn't understand why he was being so rude to her all of a sudden, acting as if she wasn't even there. It was like he was in a trance.

Katie looked around at the other kids picking apples. All of them seemed to be in some kind of trance. They were all moving like robots.

Katie stared at one of the boys near Mark, who seemed to be staring back at her. But his eyes were totally vacant, as if the life had been sucked out of them.

Suddenly, Katie remembered what her mother had read about the orchard. It used to be owned by a witch who used apples to turn all the children of Appleton into . . .

"Zombies!" Katie gasped.

"What?" Andy said.

"All those kids," Katie murmured. She could feel the color drain out of her face.

"What are you talking about?" her mother asked.

"Just look around," Katie said. "Those kids are moving like robots, and their eyes are glassy and blank."

But her mother never got the chance to look. Because suddenly, everything around them disappeared in a puff of smoke.

5

What's going on?" Katie shrieked. "Where are we?"

Katie couldn't see a thing. She couldn't even see her own hand in front of her face.

"I don't like this one bit." Andy's voice came from beside her.

Deep laughter rose from the dense mist that surrounded them.

"Dad!" Katie cried. "Mom?"

Something touched Katie's knee. She jumped back as she let out another scream.

"It's okay." Her father's voice came from across the cart. "It's just me." His hand patted her arm.

"Dad, I can't see you," Andy said nervously. "I can't see *anything*!"

"That's because we're in thick fog," Mrs. Lawrence's voice explained.

"How can we be in fog?" Katie asked. "It was a beautiful, sunny day before we came to this creepy orchard."

"They probably set up fog machines out here," her father answered. "This must be the haunted part of our hayride. Everybody get ready to be scared."

Katie was already scared. And it didn't help her nerves one bit when her mother let out a heavy sigh.

"Oh, my goodness." Mrs. Lawrence sounded very strange. Her voice seemed small and faraway. "All of a sudden, I don't feel very well."

"Neither do I," Katie's father said a moment later. His voice sounded just as odd. Tiny. Squeaky even.

"What's wrong?" Katie asked.

There was no answer.

"Mom?" Katie said.

Her mother didn't answer.

"Dad?"

He didn't answer, either.

"Stop trying to scare us," Andy ordered.

"Yeah," Katie agreed. "You guys are not funny."

There was no reply.

"Katie!" Andy said. "What's going on?"

"I don't know," Katie answered. "Maybe Owen can tell us."

But before Katie could yell to the giant scarecrow, the cart jerked to a stop. Then Katie heard voices. Strange whispering voices.

What the heck is going on now? she wondered.

"Andy?" Katie strained to see her brother through the fog. "Are you okay?"

"Yeah," he answered. Only he didn't sound okay.

Then something touched her arm. At first, Katie thought it was Andy. But it wasn't Andy.

Something was wrapping itself around Katie's arm like a snake. And it was squeezing so tightly, Katie's arm started to tingle with numbness.

Katie reached over to pull at it with her free hand.

As soon as she touched it, she realized that it wasn't a snake. It felt like a tree branch or a vine. And it was twisted around her flesh like a thick wooden rope.

"Let go of me!" Katie cried as she struggled to pull it away. But just as she started to tug, something grabbed her free hand and yanked *it* away instead.

Katie started to scream.

Her arms were being pulled in two different directions! She was sure that her whole body was going to be ripped right in two.

"Andy!" she yelled. "Help me!"

"I can't," Andy screamed back. "Something scratchy's grabbing my arms! It won't let go!"

Something cold and wet pressed down hard on the back of Katie's hand. It lasted only a second, and then the vines started unwrapping themselves from her arms. Suddenly, Katie was free.

The cart jerked forward quickly. They were moving again.

"Andy?" Katie cried in a panic. "Are you still here?"

Andy didn't have to answer Katie's question because as soon as she finished asking it, the fog started to lift and Katie could see him clearly. He was sitting next to her, trembling with fear.

"It's okay," Katie said, as much to herself as to Andy. Only it wasn't okay.

Katie and Andy had come out of the fog. But their parents were gone!

6

Mom?" Katie yelled as loud as she could. "Dad? Where are you?"

There was no answer.

Katie looked back at the fog that lay on the ground like a giant white cloud.

Her parents were somewhere in that mist. She was sure of it. Their disappearing act was probably a joke they were trying to play to make the hayride *really* scary.

"Hey, Owen," Andy screamed. "You've got to stop this cart! Our parents are gone!"

Owen paid no attention to Andy. He just kept on driving.

Katie moved closer to Owen and tapped him on the shoulder. "Excuse me," she said loudly.

Owen turned around and fixed his dark, beady eyes on Katie. He was breathing heavily. This was not a friendly scarecrow.

"Something happened to our parents!" Katie shouted at him. "You have to stop this cart!"

Katie could tell by the way Owen was glaring at her that he knew exactly what had happened. And she had the awful feeling that he wasn't going to help them, either. But she wasn't about to give up.

"Our parents are lost in the fog. We have to go back and find them," she insisted.

Owen opened his mouth and let out a groan, along with a puff of horrible breath that Katie could actually see in the chilly air. Then he turned back around and continued driving the cart forward, faster than before.

Katie reached into her jacket pocket and pulled out her cell phone. "I'll call Dad," she told Andy. But when she tapped the phone's screen, the screen didn't respond.

"Is it on?" Andy asked her.

"Yes, it's on!" Katie snapped at her brother, but she held down the power button anyway.

The phone still didn't respond.

"I charged it this morning," she told her brother.

"Well, it's dead now." Andy pointed out the obvious.

"Great." Katie sighed as she shoved the phone back into her pocket. "Now what?"

"I say we just jump off this thing and go look for them," Andy said. He looked as if he were about ready to do just that.

Katie grabbed the back of his sweatshirt. "We can't do that," she said. "What if we end up lost in the fog, too? We're just going to have to wait until we get back to the parking lot and ask someone there to help us."

"Like who?" Andy said. "Those creepy-looking ghouls?"

"They're just people in Halloween costumes," Katie reminded him. At least she *hoped* they were.

Besides, there was a much bigger problem.

"Uh-oh," Andy said. "It doesn't look like we're going back to the parking lot."

"What are you talking about?" Katie asked.

Along the path up ahead of them, another cart had stopped beside an old, run-down shack. The door of the shack was chained up and locked. The windows were covered with thick iron bars, like a prison.

There were two kids in the cart ahead of them. Katie recognized them right away.

"Andy," she gasped. "It's those two redheaded kids. The ones who got on the hayride just before we did."

They were dull and sleepy-looking, like the kids Katie had seen in the orchard.

"*Their* parents are gone, too!" Andy cried.

Katie watched in horror as the driver up ahead lifted the two zombielike children out of the cart. They hung in his arms like a pair of rag dolls as he carried them toward the shack.

"What's up with this place?" Andy whispered.

"I don't know," Katie answered. But she had the

horrible feeling that it had something to do with the story in the guidebook. If this was some kind of show, Katie didn't want to be a part of it. And if it wasn't a show, she and Andy were in serious trouble.

"Listen," she told her brother. "We've got to get out of here."

But it was too late.

The cart jerked to a stop. Owen was already out of his seat and moving toward them.

Katie shrank back against Andy as the giant scarecrow stretched out his arms, ready to grab them.

7

Run!" Katie screamed as she pushed Andy off the back of the cart. "Run fast!"

But as Andy's feet hit the ground, Owen's gigantic fingers reached for the back of Andy's collar.

"*Nooooooo!*" Katie cried.

Andy spun around and kicked Owen in the knee. Owen moaned in pain, doubling over to grab his leg.

Katie leaped off the cart and tore past him. Together she and Andy made a mad dash for the fog.

"Hold on to my jacket, so we don't lose each other," Katie ordered her brother.

Andy grabbed the back of Katie's windbreaker as they disappeared into the mist.

"Mom! Dad!" Katie screamed. "Are you out here?"

There was no reply.

"Mom! Dad!" she cried out again. "Where are you?"

"Stop screaming!" Andy said. "If Owen hears you, he'll find us!"

It was impossible to see anything in the fog. Katie couldn't even see her own hands as she waved them in front of her to keep from bumping into something.

Suddenly, the fog started to clear. In the distance, Katie could see the top of the giant shade tree in the middle of the parking lot.

"Andy, look!" Katie said, pointing ahead. "It's the parking lot. I bet Mom and Dad are waiting for us out there!"

Katie began to run faster, starting to feel relieved. Until she saw the parking lot. It was deserted.

"Hey!" Andy cried, noticing, too. "Where are all the cars?"

Katie didn't care about *all* the cars. She cared about *their* car. *Why wasn't it in the parking lot, where they left it?*

"You don't think Mom and Dad left us here, do you?" Andy asked in a panic.

"Don't be stupid," Katie told him. "Mom and Dad wouldn't leave us."

"Then where are they?" Andy demanded. "And what happened to our car?"

Katie didn't have any answers. And she didn't have any time to think, either. Dozens of ghouls with handcuffs and chains started filing out of the barn where the hayride had begun.

"It's time to chain up the children," the ghoul at the front of the line instructed the group. "Now move out!"

"Uh-oh," Andy gasped. "Something tells me we'd better get out of here before one of those ghouls sees us and chains *us* up!"

"We can't," Katie reminded him. "Not without Mom and Dad."

Just then the giant shade tree caught Katie's eye. "Do you think you can climb that tree?" she asked Andy.

"Sure," he answered. "Why?"

"If we can get to the top of it, we'll be able to see the whole orchard without anybody seeing us. Then maybe we can spot Mom and Dad," Katie said.

"Good idea," Andy agreed.

Katie and Andy dashed out from a row of hedges and ran straight for the tree. Katie hoisted Andy up to the lower branch. Then she jumped up and grabbed it herself.

Within seconds, she and Andy were safely concealed among the tree's leafy branches.

Katie watched the ground for ghouls as she continued to climb her way to the top. As she reached for the next branch, she noticed something on the back of her hand—an apple-shaped tattoo. In the center of it were the words ZOMBIE NUMBER 459.

Katie's stomach did somersaults as her mind flashed back to the hayride, back to the moment when the branches had grabbed her arms and something cold and wet had pressed down on her hand.

"Andy!" Katie cried. "I think Yaga really is trying to turn the kids at the orchard into zombies!"

"You mean like the witch in Mom's guidebook?" Andy asked.

Katie nodded as she held up her hand for Andy to see.

Andy gasped. He had an apple stamp, too. His read, ZOMBIE NUMBER 458.

"I think the candy apples had something in them," Katie said.

"But we didn't eat any apples," Andy said. Then he quickly turned pale. "Uh-oh!" he gasped.

"What?" Katie demanded.

"Mom and Dad had apple cider!" he said. "Maybe *they* turned into zombies!"

Katie shook her head. So far she hadn't seen any grown-up-looking zombies. Since the hayride, she had seen hardly any grown-ups at all, except for the ghouls. But they didn't count. "Mom and Dad are just missing," she insisted. "That's all."

Katie steadied her footing and peered out between the branches. From this high up, Katie could see the entire orchard spread out in front of her. The fog was completely gone.

She scanned every inch of the route they had taken on the hayride. There was no sign of her parents. The trail was deserted.

"Do you see them anywhere?" Andy asked.

"No," Katie answered.

"Me, neither," Andy sighed.

Then something familiar caught Katie's eye.

"Andy!" Katie swallowed hard. "Look!"

She pointed to the far edge of the property, where dozens of ghouls were gathered around a lake. But the sight of the ghouls was nowhere near as terrifying as the sight of the cars . . . the cars that used to be in the parking lot!

Katie watched in horror as a gang of green ghouls pushed her parents' car into the lake.

8

"O*ooo-wen!*"

The sound of Yaga's voice quickly pulled Katie's attention away from the lake and back toward the barn.

"We're missing zombie children numbers 458 and 459!" Yaga pushed her way past the ghouls with the chains. Peanut brittle slobber flew from her lips.

"Where are they?" Yaga bellowed. "Where are the last two zombie children? There are four hundred and fifty-nine children in Appleton, but only four hundred and fifty-seven of them are accounted for!"

Drusila scurried up beside Yaga. "I don't know *where* they are," Drusila said, "but I know *who* they are."

"Well, spit it out, you toothless troll!" Yaga demanded.

"The two Lawrence urchins," Drusila said. "I found pictures of them in their father's wallet."

Katie felt like she was going to pass out.

Yaga stared at the pictures of Katie and Andy. "Where are their parents?" she asked.

"Safely secured with all the others," Drusila answered.

"And their car?" Yaga asked.

"At the bottom of the lake," Drusila said. "No one will ever know they were here."

"Good," Yaga said. "Now all we have to do is find their two mangy children."

Just then Owen stepped through the shrubs surrounding the parking lot.

He must have been following us, Katie thought. Owen was all out of breath.

"Where are the two Lawrence children?" Yaga bellowed.

Owen didn't answer. He just stood there, trembling.

"You let them get away, didn't you?" Yaga shrieked. "I should let the cat bite out your eyes for this!"

"Yeah, yeah." Drusila snickered devilishly. "Let the cat bite out his eyes this time. That's a good idea."

Owen winced as he wiped Yaga's spit from his eyes. Katie almost felt sorry for him.

"If you don't find these two children and bring them back to me as zombies," Yaga threatened, "I *will* have your eyes bitten out. Only this time, I'll bite them out myself! Do you understand me?"

Owen nodded.

"Search the property!" Yaga commanded the others. "If I don't have all the children of Appleton by midnight tomorrow, I'll bite out *all* of your eyes!"

The ghouls took off in different directions to search for Katie and Andy.

"Come, Drusila," Yaga growled as she headed for the gift shop in the crooked old house. "We must secure the property."

Drusila shuffled away at Yaga's heels.

"Let's get out of here!" Andy whispered to Katie.

Katie shook her head. Then she put her finger to her lips and pointed downward.

Owen walked to the base of the tree.

"*Ooooooo-waaaaaay!*" Owen moaned.

Katie's heart skipped six whole beats. She and Andy were doomed. Owen was going to reach right up and grab them!

But then, to her complete surprise, Owen didn't reach up. Instead he turned around and headed off toward the woods.

Katie sat stunned for a second.

"Whew," Andy said, echoing her relief. "I can't believe he missed us."

"I know," Katie agreed. "We got lucky that time, but we'd better get out of here before someone *does* see us."

"What about Mom and Dad?" Andy asked. "We can't just leave them here."

"If Yaga and her ghouls catch us, we're dead," Katie told him. "We've got to get away. Then we can tell somebody what's going on here."

Andy nodded. It was their only hope.

Katie scanned the ground below to make sure that the coast was still clear. In the distance, the light in the gift shop was on. Katie could see Yaga and Drusila through the front window. They were standing by the door, and Yaga was opening a big metal box on the wall. Inside the box were dozens of switches. Drusila studied them as Yaga filled her mouth with more peanut brittle from the giant jar that sat on the counter. The two of them looked too busy to notice Katie and Andy.

"Listen," Katie told her brother. "The second we hit the ground, run straight for the front gates, okay?"

Andy nodded. He was ready.

Katie dropped her leg down to the branch below and began to descend. But just as she reached the next branch, a loud, shrill sound wailed through the air and shook the tree.

Katie grabbed the branch above her and held on for dear life.

"Alarms!" Andy yelled. "They're sounding the alarms!"

Dozens of floodlights snapped on all over the orchard. And from the top of the creepy old house a searchlight cut through the dusk and crisscrossed the grounds.

Within seconds, ferocious-looking dogs were let out of the barn by ferocious-looking ghouls.

"Listen up, you two Lawrence brats!"

Yaga's voice barked louder than the hounds ready to attack. It was booming through speakers, on top of the gift shop.

"You're never going to get out of here alive!" Yaga's voice cackled. "*Never!*"

Giant sparks of electricity shot up from the iron fence that surrounded the property. They crackled like bolts of lightning.

Katie turned her head as a horrible screeching sound came from the big iron gates.

Her heart sank. Yaga was right. Their only hope of escape was sliding shut.

9

Katie watched in horror as the front gates slammed closed with a shower of sparks.

"Oh, man," Andy sighed. "We're dead! There's no way we can get out of—"

Katie heard the *craaaaack* before Andy could finish.

"Oh, no!" Andy cried as the limb holding him snapped.

"Grab my hand!" Katie lunged to save her brother.

But it was too late. Andy was already falling, gathering speed as he plunged toward the ground.

Katie braced herself for the sickening thud of his body hitting the gravel below.

Andy flailed his arms, desperately trying to grab hold of the tree.

Suddenly, his shirt caught on a branch.

Katie let out her breath. "Are you okay?" she called down.

"I think so," Andy answered. He struggled to find footing. "I'm just scratched up, that's all."

Luckily, the wailing of sirens around the grounds had drowned out their screams. As Katie and Andy climbed down the tree, no one rushed over.

In fact, there didn't seem to be anyone around at all. Even Yaga and Drusila were gone. The lights in the gift shop were out.

Katie guessed that they'd headed to the orchards to join the search for her and Andy.

"We'd better get out of here now." Andy said exactly what Katie was thinking.

"I know," Katie answered. "But how?"

"Maybe we could climb over the fence," Andy suggested.

"No way!" Katie said. "Didn't you see all the sparks flying from that thing? It's electrified. If we try to climb over it, we'll be fried."

Suddenly, Katie had an idea. "All we have to do is sneak into the gift shop and find the switch that opens the gate."

"Are you nuts?" Andy said. "What if we get caught?"

"We're not going to get caught," Katie insisted. "There's nobody around to catch us. Not now, anyway." Katie grabbed Andy by the arm and raced toward the gift shop.

"What if somebody's in there?" Andy said, trying to slow their pace.

"Nobody's in there," Katie replied. "The lights are out. It's dark inside."

It was getting pretty dark *outside*, too.

Katie took a quick look behind her to make sure they were still alone as they reached the gift shop door.

Then she pushed open the creaky door and slipped inside. Andy was right behind her.

"Ew, gross," Andy said, covering his nose. "It smells disgusting in here."

Andy was right. The air inside was thick and sour-smelling.

"What kind of gift shop is this, anyway?" Andy asked.

"Who cares?" Katie shot back. "It's not like we're planning to buy anything."

"Something tells me we wouldn't want to," Andy said.

It was too dark to see much of anything. But a quick glance around told Katie that the place was full of creepy-looking stuff that smelled putrid, like rotten eggs.

"You watch outside," Katie told Andy as she stepped around the counter where Yaga's giant jar of peanut brittle stood. "Make sure no one comes this way."

Katie quickly located the metal box on the wall that Drusila had been studying.

"Oh, no," she groaned as she pulled open the box.

"What's wrong?" Andy asked.

"There are hundreds of switches in here," Katie answered. "None of them are marked. How am I supposed to know which one works the gate?"

"Just flip them all," Andy said. "Then we'll make a run for it."

Katie hesitated. It seemed dangerous—she had no idea what any of the switches controlled. But what choice did she have? She hit the first switch. The lights in the gift shop came on.

Katie snapped them back off, hoping that no one outside had noticed.

She was terrified to touch the next switch. But she forced herself to do it. It was their only hope of escape.

That one set off alarm bells *inside* the gift shop.

Katie switched it off just as quickly as the first.

"Uh, Katie," Andy began. "We've got problems."

"No kidding," Katie shot back. "I'm never going to find the right switch."

"No," Andy said. This time he sounded frantic. "I mean *big* problems!" He started backing away from the door in terror. "Owen!"

Katie looked around desperately for a back door. But there was none. She and Andy were trapped.

10

Owen came closer.

"We've got to hide!" Katie whispered.

She looked around the dark room and spotted a stack of boxes in the corner.

"Over there!" She pushed Andy toward the boxes.

They scrambled behind them just as the door began to creak open.

The sound of heavy footsteps crossed the floor, heading in their direction.

Katie and Andy held on to each other, shrinking down as low as they could.

The footsteps kept coming.

Katie was dizzy with terror. Any second now, Owen would kick the boxes aside and grab them both.

The footsteps stopped. Owen stood on the other side of the boxes. Katie could see the tips of his giant black shoes.

Katie put her hand over her mouth. She didn't even want to breathe. She didn't want to risk making any sound that Owen might hear.

All at once Owen's enormous hands reached out. But they weren't reaching for Katie or Andy. They were holding something. And he was reaching to put whatever it was high on the shelf against the back wall. Then he turned and headed back toward the door.

Katie waited to hear the door open. But that didn't happen. Instead she heard a drawer slide out. Then a loud click. And another. And another. Owen was flicking the switches.

Katie got up enough courage to peek around the side of the boxes. Owen was standing by the metal box, studying a paper he held in his hand. He flipped another switch. Then he put the paper back in the drawer under the counter and closed it.

Katie quickly ducked back behind the boxes before Owen looked in her direction. A few seconds later she heard the door creak shut.

Katie and Andy looked at each other.

"I think he's gone," Andy whispered.

Katie glanced around the room to be sure. Then she got up and headed toward the drawer in the counter.

"Katie?" Andy called after her.

"Shhh," she told him, pulling open the drawer. Inside was the paper Owen had been looking at.

"Oh, my gosh," Katie murmured.

The paper was a diagram of all the switches. Each one was clearly marked. Now all she had to do was find the switch that opened the gate.

"Katie!" Andy gasped.

She could tell by the tone of her brother's voice that something else was wrong.

Katie spun around to face the door, thinking that Owen had returned. But that wasn't it.

"Katie," Andy said again. "Look at this."

Andy stood in front of the shelves, pointing at something above him.

Lined up in rows were hundreds of tiny figures that looked like shriveled-up people. They stood on the shelf staring down at Katie and Andy with shriveled-up eyeballs!

11

They're not real!

That was what Katie tried to tell herself. But they looked so lifelike.

"What *are* these things?" Andy asked, backing away from the shelves.

"They look like dolls," Katie answered. "*Creepy* dolls."

"Well, I hope they're creepy *dead* dolls," Andy shot back. "Because they look like miniature ghoul people."

Katie forced herself to reach up and touch one of the figures with the tip of her finger. She was half expecting it to move. But when it didn't, she lifted it off the shelf.

"You see," she told her brother. "They really are just dolls."

Katie examined the shrunken-headed figure in her hand as Andy reached up to grab one himself.

"Oh, man." He flinched the second he touched it. "These things are disgusting."

Katie had to agree.

The heads of the dolls were carved out of dried, shriveled-up apples. The faces were pockmarked and lumpy where pieces of apple had been whittled away. Brown, rotting noses were chiseled between two apple-chunk cheeks, and two little nostrils were perfectly carved into tunnels.

Each doll had rigid red lips and eyeballs sunk deep into apple-hole sockets.

"Look," Andy said as he reached for another doll. "Every one of them is different."

Katie saw that he was right. No two dolls were alike. Each lumpy, gross face had its own disgusting features. Some of the dolls' noses were crooked. But others were chiseled straight down, like ski slopes, or pushed in like pug dogs', or puffed out like pigs'.

Even the hair on their heads was unique. There were different colors and styles and lengths, including a couple of dolls who were bald. Each one was dressed differently, too. There were dolls wearing suits, dresses, jeans—even pajamas. There was even a shelf full of shriveled-up ladies in puffed-up mink coats.

But the creepiest thing about all the dolls was their shriveled up eyes. Every eyeball seemed real—as if it was looking, and seeing! If the dolls didn't look so shriveled up and dead, Katie would have thought there really was some kind of life behind their eyes.

Katie quickly put the doll in her hand back on the shelf. She couldn't stand to look at it one moment longer. Besides, they had more important things to worry about.

"Come on," she said to her brother. "Put that thing down. We have to get out of here."

But Andy was mesmerized by the doll he was holding.

"Wait a minute," he said. "Who does this look like to you?" He held a plump doll in a suit up to Katie's face.

Katie pushed it away. "We don't have time for this," she told him.

"Just look at it, Katie," Andy insisted. "Please."

Finally Katie looked at the doll's face. Its chunky cheeks were puffed up like a chipmunk's. And its fat, lumpy nose stretched from one rotting ear to the other. Katie couldn't help thinking that the doll looked familiar, especially when she noticed a black mole on the top of its twisted lip.

She gasped. "It looks just like Mr. Hudson, the school principal!"

"Yeah," Andy agreed. "Pretty weird, huh?"

"*Really* weird," Katie said, shuddering as she gazed at the doll again. It looked *exactly* like Mr. Hudson.

"Look at this one," Andy told her, handing her another. "It looks like my teacher, Mrs. Cope." He pointed to the doll's head. "Her hair's even twisted into that beanie bun she wears."

Andy was right. The doll did look exactly like Mrs. Cope.

"Maybe it's a coincidence," Katie said as she nervously studied the shrunken-headed teacher in her hand.

"Oh, yeah?" Andy shot back. "Well, here's one that looks just like Mr. Gentry."

"Who's Mr. Gentry?" Katie asked.

"The butcher Mom buys our meat from," he reminded her.

"Oh, right," Katie remembered.

"Look," Andy went on. "He's wearing that bloody apron he always wears. And he's even got a little meat cleaver in his hand."

Katie glanced at the rotting stump of a butcher. Then she started to scan the shelves again. "This is so strange," she said, growing more uneasy by the second.

There were dozens of figures Katie didn't recognize. But there were dozens she did. She picked out Mrs. Gibbs, the old lady who lived next door, dressed in the same dress she'd been wearing that morning when Katie saw her picking up her newspaper. She saw the video guy from the electronics store, the gardener who took care of their lawn and raked the leaves, even the bus driver who drove them to school.

"There must be one of everybody in town," Katie said as she made her way along the shelves. "Why are they modeled after people who live in Appleton?"

"I don't know," Andy answered, picking up another pair. "Who are these two? I know I've seen them before."

Katie took a close look. She'd seen them before, too, but she couldn't remember where. Until she noticed tufts of red hair shooting out of their rotting skulls.

The rooster-headed dolls in Andy's hands were the parents of the redheaded kids on the hayride ahead of them! Their parents had been missing right after the hayride, too! Just like Katie and Andy's!

Katie's head started to reel. As she looked up to the top shelf where Owen had just placed something, the feeling got much worse. Two more dried-up dolls sat there.

Nooooooooo! Katie's brain was screaming inside her head. *This can't be!* But as Katie stared at the doll on the left, there was no way to deny what was happening. She would recognize those emerald green eyes anywhere.

12

An icy shiver went up Katie's spine as her eyes locked on the doll with the bright green eyes.

"Andy . . ." Katie managed to squeak, pointing to the top shelf.

Andy looked up. His face went pale. "It's Mom and Dad!" he gasped. "Isn't it?"

For a moment Katie couldn't speak. She'd never seen anything so horrifying. Her mother's beautiful face was squished up and rotting. Her dad's funny grin was carved into a twisted sneer.

"Our parents are appleheads!" she shrieked. "Yaga and her ghouls turned Mom and Dad into appleheads!"

"Look how little they are." Andy gulped, staring up at their shrunken parents.

"We have to get them out of here," Katie said.

But neither one of them made a move to touch their parents.

Touching the appleheads was one thing when Katie thought they were dolls. But touching applehead *people* was a whole other story. Especially when they were her parents!

"Grab them," she finally ordered her brother.

"You grab them!" Andy shot back.

Katie's heart beat faster. There were footsteps passing by outside. They had to get out of there. Now!

Katie had no choice but to reach up for her parents.

Their bodies were squishy in some places, but brittle and hard in others. Katie was afraid she was going to break them in two as she lifted them from the shelf.

"Oh, man." She choked back a sob. "Poor Mom and Dad," she said. "Look at them, Andy. They're helpless."

Katie couldn't believe she was holding her parents in her hands. And she couldn't bear the sight of their eyes looking up at her, as if they were pleading for help.

Andy stared at them. "Mom," he said nervously. "Dad? Can you hear me?"

Katie expected the figures to squiggle or squirm. But they didn't move. They didn't answer.

The roving spotlights outside reminded Katie they had to go before Yaga found them.

"Here," she said, handing their parents to her brother. "Hold them while I find the switch that opens the gate."

"Aw, geez." Andy shuddered as he took the figures. "They feel so creepy."

Katie picked up the paper with the diagram and studied it. Finally, she figured out which switch opened the gates.

"Go over to the door," she told Andy. "When the coast is clear, I'll flip the switch and we'll make a run for it. Okay?"

"Okay," Andy agreed. "But you take Mom," he said, handing her over. "I can't run with both of them."

Katie took her mother. Then she watched nervously as Andy headed to the door, opened it just a crack, and peeked outside.

"All clear," he whispered over his shoulder.

"Okay," Katie said. "We'll go on the count of three. One. Two. Three!"

The instant Katie flipped the switch, Andy burst through the door. He was off and running, with Katie right behind him.

"Run, Andy, run!" she screamed as she pushed herself to move faster.

They raced through the parking lot and headed down the gravel road. Katie could see the gates up ahead. They were beginning to open. But as they did, another siren began to blare.

Katie looked behind her, terrified that all the witches and ghouls would come after them now. The only one she saw was Yaga, running for the house. In seconds, the old witch would flip the switch and the gates would slam shut again.

"Katie!" Andy cried as he slipped through the iron bars. "Hurry!"

Katie reached the front gate just as Yaga hit the switch. Behind her, the gates came together with a clang.

"We did it!" Katie exclaimed, jumping up and down for joy. "We got away!"

"Careful!" Andy said. "You'll squish Mom!"

Katie was so excited to have escaped, she'd forgotten all about the applehead in her hand—the applehead that happened to be her mother.

Katie quickly lifted her mom to her face. "I'm sorry, Mom," she said. "I didn't mean to squeeze you so hard."

The applehead didn't reply.

"She doesn't hear you," Andy said sadly. Then he looked down at the applehead of a dad in his hands. "They probably don't even know that they're appleheads," he told Katie. "And they probably don't even know we're in trouble."

Andy was right. Their parents didn't hear them. And

they didn't see them, either. Worst of all, they couldn't help them. Katie and Andy were on their own.

Katie trembled as she peered through the darkness. Without her parents to protect her, she felt scared, even outside the orchard.

"I guess we should head home," Katie told her brother, looking up and down the dark, winding road.

"Which way is that?" Andy asked.

Katie thought about it for a second, trying to remember which way they'd turned when they drove into the orchard. "That way," she said, pointing to her left. "That's the way we came."

Katie and Andy started to walk. They were careful to stay far away from the fence that surrounded the orchard, so they wouldn't get electrocuted or grabbed.

Inside the orchard, the sirens still blared. As the searchlights crisscrossed the grounds inside the fence, they cast eerie shadows on the ground *outside,* shadows that looked like ghosts and ghouls. They made Katie and Andy jump.

"What's that?" Andy gasped, pointing to something ahead.

At first, Katie thought that Andy was just reacting to another shadowy figure. But she was wrong. The shadow Andy was pointing at was moving right toward them!

13

Someone's coming!" Katie cried in a whisper.

"They know we escaped!" Andy cried back. "And now they're out *here* looking for us!"

Katie was about to grab her brother's hand and run in the opposite direction. But then they'd be running back to the gate, where more shadowy figures were surely waiting to grab them.

"Come on." Katie pulled Andy behind a tree on the side of the road. "Just keep quiet. Don't even breathe."

Katie watched as the shadow drew closer and started to take shape.

Is it Yaga and her ghouls? she thought. *Or Owen?*

A second later her question was answered.

The figures approaching weren't witches or ghouls. They were kids. Kids that Katie recognized!

"It's Christine and Laura and Jill! The girls that invited me to the Halloween party!" Katie exclaimed. "What are they doing here?" Katie stepped out from behind the tree. "Christine!" she called out.

But Christine didn't answer.

"Hey, guys!" Katie rushed toward them. "Stop!"

None of them did. They just kept walking toward the front gate as if Katie didn't exist.

"Wait!" she cried, running after them. "Don't go in there. There's an evil witch and ghouls in that orchard. See—they turned my mom and dad into appleheads," she went on, holding up her mother. "And they tried to turn Andy and me into zombies!"

None of her friends reacted. They just kept moving toward the gate. Katie's heart stopped. *Her friends were acting like zombies!*

"Come on," Katie said, tugging Andy along. "Let's just get out of here!"

Katie and Andy ran. And ran. And ran. They didn't stop until they reached the end of the dark, winding road.

"We're almost there," Katie panted, clutching a cramp in her side. "Look," she told Andy. "We're on Main Street. Just another mile or so and we'll be home."

Andy was gasping for air. "Can't we rest for a second?"

"No," Katie said, taking off again. "We've got to go home and call the police."

By the time Katie turned onto their street, the pain in her side had spread to every muscle in her body. But she wasn't about to stop. Not when safety was just a few feet away.

But as Katie and Andy turned into the driveway of the familiar old house with the dark gray shutters, Katie's knees buckled beneath her.

Home wasn't a safe place to be after all.

14

The house had been attacked.

Broken eggs and shaving cream were smeared all over the windows. Toilet paper was draped from tree to tree like giant spider webs. And the fifty-pound pumpkin that Katie and Andy had carved with their father was smashed into a thousand pieces in the driveway.

"Somebody trashed our house!" Andy cried. "Do you think it was the ghouls from the orchard?"

"No." Katie shook her head as she remembered what day it was. "Tomorrow's Halloween, so tonight's mischief night," she reminded her brother. "It was probably a bunch of stupid kids." At least she hoped that's all it was. "Let's get inside before somebody tries to attack *us*," she said, running for the front porch.

At the front door Katie let out a groan. "It's locked!" She dug through her pockets, frantically looking for her keys. "Please tell me you have your house keys with you," she told Andy.

Andy shook his head.

"Terrific," Katie said. "Now we can't get in."

"Wait a minute," Andy said. "Dad always puts his keys in his pants pocket!"

"Look at how small Dad is!" Katie snapped at her brother. "Even if his keys *are* in his pocket, you know how small they have to be? There's no way they're going to open this door."

"Maybe the back door's unlocked," Andy suggested.

They went around to the back of the house, but that one was sealed tightly, too.

"Check the windows," Katie said.

Katie and Andy made their way around the house trying every window there was. None of them budged until they got to the one over the kitchen sink. That window slid right open.

Katie sent Andy in first.

Andy leaned through the window, put his parents down on the counter, then climbed in himself.

"Oh, no!" he wailed a second later. "Dad rolled off the counter onto the floor!"

"Is he hurt?" Katie asked, squeezing through the window after her brother.

"How should I know?" Andy replied. "He's an applehead!"

Andy picked up their father and brushed him off. "He looks okay," he announced. Then he picked up their mom and stood her up on the counter before she rolled to the floor, too.

"We'd better put them somewhere safe before they get smushed," Katie said, climbing down from the counter herself.

"Like where?" Andy asked.

Katie noticed the fruit bowl on the kitchen table. "Put them in there," she told Andy, pointing to it.

"The fruit bowl?" Andy asked. "You want me to put Mom and Dad in a fruit bowl?!"

"Where else should we put them?" Katie asked.

"I don't know," Andy shot back. "Maybe we should put them in the den so they can watch TV."

"Appleheads can't watch TV," Katie said. "Put them in the bowl with the other fruit. At least they'll be safe there."

"I guess," Andy agreed finally. Carefully, he put their parents in the bowl, next to the bananas.

Katie picked up the mobile phone on the kitchen desk. She checked the list of important numbers that her mother kept on the refrigerator and started to dial.

"What are you doing?" Andy asked.

"Calling the police," Katie said. "I'm going to tell them about the orchard."

"Appleton Police," a man's voice said. "This is Officer Walker."

"My name is Katie Lawrence," Katie blurted. "My brother and I need help right away."

"What seems to be the problem?" the officer asked calmly.

"This afternoon my parents took us out sightseeing around town," Katie started to ramble nervously. "And we ended up at the Appleton Orchard, which was supposed to be charcoal. At least according to my mother's guidebook," she went on. "It said that a bunch of angry parents burned it to the ground three hundred years ago after some evil witch turned all the kids into zombies with poisoned apples." Katie stopped to take a breath.

"I see," the officer said, sounding suspicious.

"Only it wasn't burned to the ground," Katie continued. "The orchard was open. And there really was an evil witch there. Her name is—"

The officer interrupted Katie. "Listen, kid." He sounded stern. "This line is for emergencies, not prank calls."

"This is an emergency!" Katie said. "The evil witch turned our parents into appleheads!"

"I thought you just told me that the evil witch turned all the kids into zombies," the officer shot back.

"She did!" Katie told him. "The adults are appleheads; the kids are zombies. I have a stamp on my hand to prove it!" she added.

The officer sighed loudly. "Where are your parents now?" he asked.

"Right here," Katie answered. "In the fruit bowl."

"Well, why don't you put one of them on the phone," he said.

"I can't!" Katie shouted into the receiver. "I told you, they're both appleheads!"

"I'm not so sure your mom and dad would be too happy to hear you call them that," the officer scolded. "Prank, or no prank."

"This isn't a prank," Katie insisted. "There really is an evil witch. And my parents really *are* appleheads!"

"Yeah, yeah," the officer said. "And the last kid that called here tonight told me *his* parents were abducted by aliens. Now, I know that it's mischief night," he went on. "But the police department doesn't take kindly to practical jokes."

"This isn't a joke," Katie said.

"No, it's not," the officer agreed. "Tying up the police department's phone lines is not a joke. And if you call here again, I'm going to send some officers out there to talk to your parents."

"B-but . . ." Katie sputtered.

"But nothing," the officer cut in. "Have a happy Halloween." With a click the line went dead. Katie stood holding the phone in her hand.

"What did he say?" Andy asked.

"He didn't believe a word I told him," Katie said. "He thought I was making some kind of prank call."

"Maybe I should call him, too," Andy said. "I bet he'll believe us if I say the same thing."

Katie doubted it, but she figured it was worth a shot. She was about to hand her brother the phone when, with a gasp, she dropped it. Someone was moving around outside the sliding glass doors in the kitchen!

The glass was covered with shaving cream, but Katie could definitely see someone. Someone big. Someone she had hoped never to see again!

Katie screamed as the horrible creature with the basketball-sized head pressed its painted-on face up against the glass. Owen, the scarecrow, was staring at her!

15

Owen!" Katie shrieked as she pointed to the sliding glass doors.

"Where?" Andy spun around to look. But Owen's face had disappeared.

"He was there a second ago!" Katie insisted. "I saw him!"

Someone pounded on the front door.

"Aaaaaaagh!" Andy screamed. "He's trying to break in!"

Then the pounding stopped. That scared Katie even more.

"Uh-oh!" Katie gasped. "He's coming around to the kitchen again! Quick," she said, pulling her brother into the foyer. "We have to get upstairs."

Katie and Andy tore up the steps and into Katie's room. They slid under the bed as fast as they could.

For a good ten minutes, they lay in the darkness, listening. But there was nothing to hear.

"You think he left?" Andy finally whispered.

"I hope so," Katie answered, starting to feel a little bit better. She crawled out from under the bed. Then she heard voices drifting up into her room from outside.

Andy heard them, too. He gulped. "Who is that? Ghouls?"

"I don't know," Katie replied, terrified.

But the voices drifting through Katie's bedroom window weren't ghoul voices at all.

"It's kids!" Katie exclaimed a moment later. "Listen, Andy. They're just kids, laughing and shouting."

Andy was sitting on the bed biting his fingernails. "Are you sure?"

"Yes," Katie said, patting his shoulder. "They're

probably doing Halloween mischief." Then she had an idea. "Maybe they can help us."

But as Katie crept over to the window, she started to have second thoughts. Maybe the kids who were laughing and shouting were kids from the orchard. Zombies who'd come with Owen!

A loud bang outside made Katie jump. Slowly, she leaned over to peek out the window. Owen was nowhere in sight. But on the lawn was a group of kids running away from the house.

Katie wanted to open her window to call to them. But she was too afraid that Owen was hiding somewhere nearby.

Andy stood next to her. "Maybe we should call the police again," he suggested.

Katie shook her head. "They won't believe us." Then she remembered something Officer Walker had said. "Wait a minute!" she said. "You're right. We *should* call the police back! That way they'll think it's another prank call. And then they really will send somebody out to talk to Mom and Dad!"

"Have you lost it, or what?" Andy said. "The police can't talk to Mom and Dad. They're appleheads!"

"I know," Katie shot back. "But once the police get here, we can prove to them that we're not making up stories."

Katie reached for the phone and dialed. Once again she got connected to Officer Walker.

"Appleton Police." His voice came over the line. "Officer Walker speaking."

"This is Katie Lawrence again," Katie said into the receiver. "My brother and I still need the police."

"Oh, really?" Officer Walker didn't sound amused. "What happened now?" he asked. "Did the evil witch turn *you* into an applehead? Or did she turn your brother into a zombie?"

"Neither," Katie told him. "But Owen, the evil scarecrow, is outside our house! And he's trying to break in!"

"Okay, kid," Officer Walker said. "I've had enough of this nonsense. What's your address? I'm coming out there myself to talk to your parents."

"Good," Katie said. "We're at twenty-four Applegate Drive," she told him. "Hurry!"

As the line went dead, Katie high-fived her brother. "They're coming!" she exclaimed triumphantly. "Now all we have to do is wait."

Katie and Andy waited nervously inside the house until they saw blue and red lights flashing through the darkness outside.

"They're here!" Katie cried.

She and Andy raced into the kitchen and scooped up their parents from the fruit bowl.

As Katie pulled open the front door, she saw the police car turn into the driveway. Then she saw something else.

"I don't believe it!" Katie said. "Those cops just ran over our mailbox!"

"Who cares." Andy pushed her out of the house. "At least they're here!"

Katie and Andy dashed across the lawn toward the car. It was sitting up on the curb, right where the mailbox used to be. Its blue and red lights were still flashing like crazy.

"Hey!" Andy said as they reached the car. "There aren't any cops in this car."

Katie didn't see anybody inside, either.

But that's impossible, she thought.

"Hey, Officers." Katie tapped on the window.

No one responded.

"Where did they go?" Katie mumbled as she pressed her nose against the glass to get a better look.

But she wasn't prepared for what she saw.

16

The policemen are appleheads!" Katie yelled to Andy.

"What do you mean, the policemen are appleheads?" Andy asked.

"Look!" Katie pointed inside the car.

Two tiny applehead policemen sat on the front seat of the police car. They were dressed in uniform, complete with guns and badges.

Andy smashed his face against the window to see.

"Oh, man," he cried a second later. "No wonder they crashed right into our mailbox! They can't even reach the steering wheel!"

"Wait a minute," Katie said, thinking out loud. "There's no way they could have been appleheads when they left the police station. Appleheads can't drive a police car. They're too short to even climb in."

"So they turned into appleheads after they started driving," Andy reasoned.

"Yeah," Katie said. "Right before they smashed into our mailbox."

"But what made them shrink?" Andy asked.

"I don't know," Katie answered. "But I'm going to find out."

Katie opened the door to the police car. Immediately she noticed the name on the badge the driver was wearing. Officer Walker.

"He's the one I talked to on the phone," she told Andy. "He definitely wasn't an applehead then."

Katie stuck her head in farther.

"What are you looking for?" Andy asked.

"A clue," Katie replied. "Maybe something in this car turned them into appleheads."

Katie saw exactly what it was. And she smelled it, too.

"Look!" She pointed to two overturned coffee mugs. The contents had puddled on the floor of the car. "The policemen were drinking apple cider!"

"Do you think Yaga gave it to them?" Andy asked.

That's exactly what Katie was thinking. *Only how did Yaga do it?*

Suddenly she had a terrible thought. "What if Yaga and her ghouls have figured out a way to poison *all* the apples in Appleton?" she asked.

"You mean like in all the stores?" Andy asked.

Katie nodded.

Andy turned pale. "Then everybody who drinks apple cider or eats apples will turn into an applehead or a zombie?"

Katie nodded again, feeling as terrified as Andy looked.

"So how come there weren't any applehead kids at the orchard?" Andy asked.

"I don't know," Katie answered. "Maybe Yaga's poison works one way on adults, and another way on kids."

A strong burst of wind tore through the trees. A moan echoed through the air.

"Uh-oh." Andy was startled. "Is that Owen?"

Katie didn't know. What she did know was that she wanted to be back under her bed.

"Come on," she cried as she slammed the squad car door and took off across the lawn. "We'd better get back inside and lock all the doors!"

"What about the policemen?" Andy asked as he raced up behind her. "Should we put *them* in the fruit bowl, too?"

"We'll get them tomorrow when it's light out," Katie said as she ran through the front door.

Once Katie and Andy were safely inside with the doors and windows bolted, Katie started to think again.

"What if Yaga really is the same witch that Mom was reading about in the guidebook?" she asked Andy as she paced the kitchen floor.

"What if?" Andy asked, confused.

"Well then maybe we could find out more about her," Katie said.

"Yeah, how?" Andy wanted to know. "We can't go online because Mom set up those stupid parental controls. And Dad can't sign us on because he's sitting in the fruit bowl!"

"Ugh!" Katie sighed. Andy was right. Their computer would be useless. "We'll have to go to the library," she told her brother. "There are all kinds of old newspapers and magazines to search through there. Maybe we can even find a book about her."

"How's that going to help us?" Andy asked.

"If we can find out about her, maybe we can figure out a way to stop her," Katie suggested.

"Good idea," Andy agreed. "Is the library open now?"

"No," Katie said. "We'll have to wait until tomorrow. For now, I think we should try to get some sleep."

"Yeah, right," Andy said. "Like I'm really going to be able to close my eyes with Owen lurking around out there."

"Come on," Katie said, heading out of the kitchen. "We'll both stay in my room. Under the bed."

Katie looked back at the fruit bowl before she switched off the kitchen light. "Good night, Mom. Good night, Dad. I love you."

"Me, too," Andy added. Then they headed up to Katie's room and crawled under the bed.

It was going to be a very long night.

17

Katie didn't sleep a wink. She just lay there, under the bed, listening to the wind howl and the windows rattle.

Finally it was daylight.

Even though Katie was exhausted, she and Andy had to get to the library as soon as it opened. She dragged herself up and headed downstairs.

Andy had already gone down to the kitchen, and when Katie arrived, he was eating a bowl of cereal. Sitting at the table facing him were their applehead parents.

"Happy Halloween," Katie grumbled.

It was supposed to have been a fun day. There was going to be a party at school, a big parade, and another party at Christine's house, too. But right now all Katie could think about was getting her parents back to normal.

"We're going to have to call school," Andy reminded her. "So they know we're not coming today. Just pretend that you're Mom and tell them we're sick."

"What a lousy reason to have a day off," Katie said as she picked up the phone. But she didn't dial. Not yet. She had to practice first.

"Hello, this is Mrs. Lawrence," Katie said, disguising her voice. "Katie and Andrew's mother." She looked over at Andy. "Do I sound like Mom?" she asked.

"You sound more like her than I would," he answered.

It was hardly the reassurance she wanted to hear. But it was going to have to do.

Katie started to dial. She was so nervous she could barely breathe. She'd never missed a single day of school before. And now she was calling up, pretending to be her mother.

Katie chewed on her thumbnail as she waited, hoping she wouldn't get caught. With each ring she got more and more nervous, knowing that at any moment someone was going to answer.

But after ten rings she started to wonder. *Why isn't anyone picking up?*

"Nobody's there," she told Andy as she paced the floor.

"Maybe they're all at the orchard," Andy said. "Don't you remember? We saw the principal there, and my teacher, too. Maybe there was like a teacher conference at the orchard or something this weekend. And maybe they're *all* appleheads!"

Katie stared at him. What if Andy was right? "We've got to get to that library!" she said, hanging up the phone. "Now!"

Andy got up from the table. "What should we do with them?" he asked, pointing at their parents.

"Leave them here," Katie answered, grabbing a set of house keys from the kitchen drawer. "They'll be safer at home than with us."

Andy nodded, then he followed Katie outside.

The police car was still in front of the house with its lights flashing. When Katie looked in, she saw the two applehead policemen still sitting on the front seat.

The rest of the neighborhood was deserted.

"Even Mr. Jones isn't out today," Andy said.

Katie looked across the street to where the old man lived. Mr. Jones was always out on the front porch in the morning, waving to everyone who passed. But to-day Mr. Jones was nowhere to be seen.

Without saying anything to Andy, Katie ran across the street and up the lawn to Mr. Jones's porch.

A little applehead doll sat on Mr. Jones's porch swing. Katie immediately recognized the old man's white hair and glasses. Beside him on the swing sat a cup of apple cider.

"Oh, no!" Andy cried as he came up beside Katie. "Not him, too."

"We've got to find out what's going on," Katie said. "And how to stop it."

She turned and headed back down the street toward the library.

It was only eight blocks from their house to the library, but it felt like the longest walk of Katie's life.

The other streets were empty, too. There wasn't a soul to be seen. Katie was beginning to worry that she and Andy were the only two people in Appleton who weren't zombies or appleheads yet.

But just as they started up the walkway to the library, they saw someone else. It was a fireman hanging a banner about the Halloween parade over the library door.

"Maybe we can get him to help us," Andy said.

Katie thought about it for a second, then decided it wasn't a good idea. "He won't believe us any more than the police did," she told her brother. "Let's try to get some information first."

The fireman didn't even notice them as they walked past him into the library.

Katie went straight to the librarian's desk. But there

was no librarian, just an applehead sitting in the chair. A cup of cider was on the desk in front of her.

"How are we going to find a book now?" Andy asked. "There's nobody to help us."

"Follow me," Katie told him.

She knew exactly where to look for what they needed. The books about the history of Appleton were all the way at the back of the library. Katie knew that because she'd done a report about the founding fathers of the town. She only hoped there was some information in one of those books that could help them now.

"What are we looking for?" Andy asked as he followed Katie into the history aisle.

"I don't know," she answered. She didn't even try to keep her voice down. There was no point. They were the only ones in the library anyway.

"Try to find something about the orchard," Katie told Andy as she began scanning the shelves herself.

A title caught her eye right away. "Look at this," she said, nudging Andy. "*The History of Appleton Orchard.*"

It was a big, fat book. "There's got to be something in this book that will help us," she said, reaching for it.

She had to believe that this was true. She was even beginning to feel a little hopeful until she pulled the book off the shelf.

Through the space where the book had sat, Katie could see into the next aisle. Something moved, catching her eye.

Balanced on her tiptoes, Katie peeked through the space to see what it was.

But just as she did, a monster-sized hand shot out from between the books on the shelf and reached for her throat!

18

The book in Katie's hands fell to the floor with a thud. Katie jumped back from the shelf, screaming in terror.

"It's Owen!" she cried. "We've got to get out of here!"

Katie pushed Andy down the narrow aisle, and tore off ahead of him. "Run!" she yelled at the top of her lungs.

Owen came after them. He headed toward the front doors of the library to block their escape.

"Oooog," he grunted at them.

Katie turned to her left and darted into the children's room. Andy was right behind her.

"How do we get out of here?" Andy cried.

Katie didn't answer. She just kept going. She ran through the first door she saw. She was already through it before she realized that the sign on the door said KEEP OUT.

Katie tried to turn around, but Andy was right behind her, pushing her forward. She gasped as the two of them began to topple down a staircase. Katie was on the fourth step down when she finally managed to regain her balance.

Behind her Andy came to a stop, too.

"Keep going!" he said.

The footsteps were coming closer and closer as Katie and Andy raced down the steps, taking them two at a time. The steps led down to the basement. It was a dark, dingy place. The air was so musty, Katie began to sneeze. The sneezes sounded like explosions as they bounced off the cinder-block walls and echoed all around them.

"Shhh," Andy said, slapping his hand over Katie's mouth. "With all the noise you're making, he'll find us for sure."

The door at the top of the stairs opened slowly.

Katie turned around, frantically trying to find some way to escape from Owen. But there was no way out of that basement besides the stairs. The few grimy windows in the room were up high, and they were far too small for a person to squeeze through. There was no question about it. They were trapped.

19

"Over here," Andy whispered suddenly. He motioned toward a huge file cabinet in the corner.

The two of them ducked behind the file cabinet as Owen flicked on the light.

Katie held her breath, too scared to move. The room was silent.

What is Owen doing? she wondered.

As if to answer, a loud crash echoed right over her head. It sounded as though Owen had jumped up on top of the file cabinet.

Katie and Andy both screamed as they held on to one another for dear life.

It's over, Katie thought. *Owen's got us now.*

Katie was hoarse by the time she realized no one had grabbed them. Her scream trailed off as she looked up at the top of the file cabinet. Owen wasn't there.

Surely he knew where they were.

So where was he? And what was *he doing?*

Katie put her hand over Andy's mouth to quiet him. When he was silent, she put her finger to her lips to signal him to stay quiet. He nodded. Then, slowly and cautiously, Katie raised herself up until she could just barely see over the top of the file cabinet.

There was no sign of Owen.

Katie stood a little higher.

He was gone. She was sure of it.

She was about to heave a sigh of relief. Then she saw what had crashed on top of the file cabinet.

It wasn't Owen. But it was a present from him.

20

What is that?" Andy demanded. He stood up and came over to Katie. Together they stared at the thing Owen had left.

Slowly Katie reached out and picked up the small leatherbound book from the top of the file cabinet.

"It looks like it's a million years old," Andy said.

Katie nodded. The book's leather was cracked, and the edges of the pages were crumbling. Katie was afraid that if she tried to open it, the whole thing would fall apart.

She looked on the cover and spine for a title. But

there wasn't one. Then, very carefully, Katie opened the book to the first page.

It was a diary.

"Wow," Katie said, scanning the first page. "This diary was written a hundred years ago," she told Andy.

"Whose is it?" Andy asked.

Katie began reading aloud.

"'My name is Martha Grant. I am twelve years old. I hope that someday, a hundred years from now, somebody reads this diary.'"

"Look at the date!" Andy exclaimed, pointing to the top of the page. "That's exactly today! She wrote this on October thirty-first—a hundred years ago!"

Katie nodded. "This is too weird," she said. Then she went on reading.

"'Something terrible has happened in Appleton. A horrible witch named Yaga appeared at the orchard the day before Halloween. She poisoned all the town's apples. And she used them to turn the adults into shriveled-up applehead dolls and the children into zombies.'"

"We were right!" Andy declared. "Yaga's poison works differently on grown-ups than it does on kids!"

"If only Mom and Dad hadn't . . ." Katie's voice trailed off. A lump rose in her throat.

"So what happened to everybody?" Andy asked, sounding afraid to hear the answer.

Katie forced herself to read on.

" 'Tonight, at the stroke of midnight, the orchard began to burn. Yaga burst into flames and disappeared. At first I was relieved. But as soon as Yaga was gone, everyone else within the gates of the orchard disappeared, too. Even the zombie children and the applehead adults. My own brother and parents have disappeared. Appleton is completely deserted. I am all alone.' "

Katie stopped reading, and she and Andy just looked at one another. Katie could tell that Andy was thinking the same thing she was. If they didn't do something to save their parents and their friends, they would end up just like Martha Grant—alone in a ghost town.

21

Why is Yaga doing this?" Andy asked. Katie scanned the pages of Martha Grant's diary, looking for the answer. It didn't take her long to find it.

"'Two hundred years ago today,'" Katie read on, "'several children from Appleton died after eating apples from Yaga's orchard. Angry parents stormed the grounds and set fire to Yaga's orchard. Yaga walked into the flames before the angry parents could bring her to trial. Before she disappeared in the flames, she put a curse on the town. She vowed that she would return to Appleton every hundred years to wreak her revenge.'"

"We've got to stop her," Andy declared.

Katie agreed. *But how?* she wondered. She kept reading silently, hoping to find the answer in the pages of Martha Grant's diary.

"We need help," Andy went on. "I think we should go to the police station. We can show them the diary. Then maybe they'll believe us."

"Not yet," Katie said, without taking her eyes off the page. "I don't want to hand this diary over to anyone until I've read every word."

Katie was sure that there was important information in the diary; maybe even a way to get rid of Yaga once and for all. Why else would Martha Grant have written it?

Katie was right, Martha Grant did have a plan to get rid of Yaga. There were only two problems with it. Since no one had ever tried it before, it might not work. And it was very, very dangerous. But it was their only hope.

"Come on," Katie said to Andy as she closed the diary and headed for the stairs. "We don't have much time. And there's a lot we have to do."

"Why do you think Owen gave us this diary?" Andy asked as they went up the stairs.

"I've been wondering that, too," Katie said.

"Maybe he's trying to help us," Andy suggested.

Katie shook her head. "If Owen's trying to help us, then why did he let Mom and Dad drink the poisoned apple cider in the first place? And why did he grab at my throat before?"

Andy shrugged. "I don't know," he admitted.

Owen was up to no good. Katie was sure of it. "He probably just wants to scare us even worse than we already are," she told Andy.

"Well, he's doing a really good job of it," Andy replied.

At the top of the stairs, Katie pushed the door open a crack and peeked into the library. No one was there.

She stuck her head out and looked around. Still no one.

"Let's go," she said to Andy.

They moved quickly, keeping careful watch around

them. They made it through the children's room, through the lobby, and out the front door.

The cool, fresh air felt good, especially after the dark, musty basement. Katie sucked in a deep breath and felt herself start to relax a little. Now that they had a plan, at least there was hope.

But then she saw something in front of her. Something as horrifying as anything she'd seen so far.

22

Ewwwwwwwww, gross!" Andy cried at the horrible sight.

The fireman who had been hanging the banner outside the library had fallen off his ladder. But that wasn't the worst of it. Now he was an applehead. And a squirrel was nibbling away at him!

"Shoo!" Katie hollered at the squirrel, stomping her foot on the pavement to scare it away.

It didn't work. The squirrel looked up at her for a second. Then it went right back to munching on the fireman's head.

"Oh, man." Andy cringed. "We can't let that squirrel eat his brains out!"

"Throw something at him," Katie suggested in a panic.

Andy bent down to snatch up a pebble from the ground. Then he tossed it at the squirrel, hitting the animal in the hind leg.

The startled squirrel jumped two feet in the air, let out an angry squeak, then took off like a shot.

Andy headed toward the applehead fireman.

Katie hung back. She didn't want to see what the squirrel had done to him. She was afraid that the squirrel had nipped off his nose or nibbled out his eyes.

"It's not so bad," Andy told her as he picked up the fireman. "The squirrel just took a little chunk out of the back of his head." Andy held out the applehead for Katie to see.

But Katie didn't want to see. "Just cover it up with his hair," she told Andy.

Andy did just that. Then he started to place the fireman back on his ladder.

"No." Katie stopped him. "Bring him with us. We'll show him to the police. With him and the diary, they'll have to believe us."

"Good thinking," Andy agreed. "Let's go."

The police station was right across the street from the library.

The two of them dashed down the walkway in front of the library and paused to look both ways before crossing the street.

No cars, Katie thought. That was odd. There was always plenty of traffic in town. But not today. *Why?*

Katie didn't have much time to think about it.

A moment later, she and Andy burst through the front doors of the police station like a S.W.A.T. team.

The place was empty.

"Hello," Katie called out.

The only answer she got was the eerie echo of her own voice.

"Is anybody here?" she called louder as she and Andy moved into the front office.

"Look," Andy said, pointing to the chair behind one of the desks.

Before she even looked over the top of the desk, Katie knew what she was going to see. An applehead policeman.

Every chair at every desk in the front office was occupied by an applehead. And sitting on every desk was a cup of cider.

"Isn't there anybody in this town who doesn't drink apple cider?" Katie groaned. "Come on," she said, moving down the corridor. "Let's check out the rest of the station."

Andy followed.

They went into every room until they reached the last office in the building.

"She did it," Andy said as he laid the applehead fireman on the applehead police chief's desk. "Yaga's already poisoned the whole town."

"No." Katie refused to believe it. "There's got to be someone left."

As if to prove her point, a door creaked open. There was the sound of footsteps.

"See?" she told Andy. She was about to call out, but something stopped her.

It was the footsteps. They didn't sound right.

Katie quickly put a finger to her lips to signal Andy to stay quiet. Then she listened.

The footsteps were coming closer. And there were lots of them. But it didn't sound like people walking normally.

Katie looked around the office for someplace to hide. She found a closet, and she and Andy managed to duck into it in the nick of time.

Katie was pulling the closet door shut when the shuffling feet came into the office.

As Katie caught a peek of who the feet belonged to, she was glad that she and Andy had stayed quiet. It wasn't help that had arrived. It was zombies.

23

Katie and Andy stayed hidden inside the closet until they no longer heard any movement in the room.

"I think they're gone," Katie whispered.

She pushed open the door and peered out. The room was empty. Nervously, she crept out of the closet.

"What were they doing here?" Andy whispered, coming out behind her.

Katie wasn't sure. But she had a hunch.

"Look," she said, pointing to the desk. "The fireman is gone. So is the police chief. The zombies must have taken them."

"Why?" Andy asked.

Katie shrugged. She didn't know, but it didn't matter right now. All that mattered was finding another real person in Appleton.

"Let's go to the fire station," Katie suggested. "Maybe there's someone there."

Andy nodded.

They headed back through the building toward the exit. Every office *really* was empty now. All the zombies were gone. So were all the appleheads.

When they opened the door to go outside, Katie and Andy stopped dead in their tracks. The town was full of zombie children! They shuffled along, up and down the streets, going from building to building. In their arms were dozens of appleheads.

"Oh, my gosh," Andy breathed. "Do you think Yaga sent all these zombies out to get all the appleheads?"

Katie nodded. "We've got to get home," she said in a panic. "Before the zombies get Mom and Dad, too."

"Unless they've already got them!" Andy added.

Katie and Andy took off down the street.

Surprisingly, the zombies didn't pay any attention to them. They were too busy collecting appleheads.

The farther away from the center of town they got, the fewer zombies they saw.

"Maybe they haven't gotten to our neighborhood yet," Katie said hopefully. Or maybe they'd already been there.

Katie and Andy turned onto Applegate Drive.

The muscles in Katie's legs were burning, but the instant she saw her house, she pushed herself to run even faster. Andy stayed right beside her.

There wasn't a zombie in sight as they dashed up the porch steps. Katie fumbled nervously with the keys. Finally, she managed to get the front door open.

"Mom!" she called out. "Dad!"

Of course there was no answer. Katie didn't really expect one.

She ran for the kitchen with Andy right behind her. She stopped short in the doorway, her eyes fixed on the kitchen table.

Andy crashed into her.

"Are they . . ." Andy didn't finish the question.

"They're still here!" Katie exclaimed.

Katie was relieved her parents were okay. But she knew her problems were far from over.

They still had to face Yaga. And they had to do it alone.

Katie sat down at the kitchen table and started to read Martha Grant's diary again before they headed back to the orchard, to be sure that she hadn't missed a thing.

There was only one way that Katie and Andy might save Appleton and their parents. Katie stared at the words on the page: *To defeat Yaga you must turn her own magic against her. Give her a taste of her own poison.*

But how?

24

Hurry," Katie said as she and Andy pedaled their way through the darkness.

It had been well past nine o'clock when Katie and Andy got on their bikes and headed for the orchard. Katie was terrified that they would never make it in time. According to Martha Grant's diary, they had to defeat Yaga before midnight, and midnight was less than three hours away. And they still had to figure out a way to sneak into the orchard without being seen.

Katie and Andy were dressed all in black. Both wore baggy cargo pants with deep side pockets. In the left pocket, each of them carried one of their parents. In the right pocket, they each held a weapon—a squirt bottle of poison cider which they'd collected from mugs left around town. It was what they'd use to try to defeat Yaga.

"Are you sure your plan is going to work?" Andy asked as he struggled to keep up.

"Of course it's going to work," Katie said. She hoped she sounded braver than she felt.

The two of them rode on in silence. A few minutes later, the iron bars surrounding the orchard came into view.

Katie and Andy slammed on their brakes.

Katie couldn't believe it. She'd spent all night trying to figure out how to get past the gates, and now they were wide open!

But, as it turned out, that wasn't very good news. A bunch of ghouls were standing near the entrance, observing the long line of zombie kids that was filing through.

"Oh, no," Katie mumbled. "What are we going to do? There's no way we can get past those ghouls." As she stared at the line, she suddenly had an idea. "Hey, Andy. Do you think you can pretend to be a zombie kid?"

"No way, Katie," he said, shaking his head. "We're not getting in that line!"

"We have to," Katie insisted. "It's the only way we'll get inside. Don't you want to help Mom and Dad?" she pleaded.

Andy couldn't say no to that.

Katie's legs shook as she climbed off her bike and ditched it on the side of the road. She and Andy were about to enter the orchard. But would they ever make it out again?

Katie waited for Andy to get off his bike, and then she started moving toward the line of zombies.

"Wait." Andy stopped her.

"What now?" she asked impatiently. They didn't have any time to waste.

"Look at those zombie kids," he said. "They're all carrying appleheads."

Andy was right. Every single zombie kid had at least one applehead in his or her hands. If Katie and Andy weren't carrying appleheads, too, somebody would notice.

She reached into her pocket and produced her own applehead. "I'll carry Mom," she told Andy. "And you carry Dad. That way we'll blend right in."

Slowly, Andy reached into his own pocket and pulled out his father. "I'm not going to let anything bad happen to you," he said to the applehead. "I promise."

Katie hoped it was a promise they could keep.

"Now just follow my lead and act like a zombie," she told him.

Katie and Andy shuffled over to the back of the line, trying to walk like the rest of the kids.

"This isn't going to work," Andy whispered in a panic.

"Shut up," Katie whispered back. "Zombie kids don't talk!"

"And they don't shake like you're shaking, either," Andy shot back.

Katie *was* shaking. Especially when she saw what was going on at the front of the line.

"Andy." It was Katie's turn to panic. "Do you still have your zombie stamp?"

Andy looked at his hand. "Yeah," he answered. "Why?"

"Because the ghouls are checking everybody's hands for the stamp," she said.

"Uh-oh," Andy whispered. "What if those ghouls remember our numbers? What if they realize we're the kids who were missing?"

"No way," Katie said. "Those stupid ghouls will never remember the numbers on our hands."

Only the ghoul that was waiting to check Katie's and Andy's hands wasn't a ghoul at all. It was a scarecrow. And Katie was sure that *this* scarecrow would definitely remember their faces.

25

Owen looked Katie right in the eye.

She could feel her whole body tremble as she waited for him to grab her and turn her over to Yaga.

But Owen didn't even look at Katie's stamp as she held up her hand. He just stared hard into her eyes.

Katie had to force herself to keep moving. She could feel Andy plodding along behind her. Owen had let them pass. Why?

Although Katie desperately wanted to turn around to see if Owen was following them, she didn't dare. The ghouls would notice for sure.

But she couldn't dwell on Owen, either. There were bigger problems up ahead.

Drusila, the witch, stood behind a high basket. As the zombie children passed her they were dropping their applehead people into her basket.

Katie held on to her mother so tightly, she was afraid she might crush her.

No way, Katie thought. *I can't drop Mom into that basket!* Who knew what would happen to her parents once they got into Drusila's clutches?

Katie tried frantically to think of something to do. She was only two zombies away from Drusila's basket.

The zombie in front of Katie dropped her appleheads into the basket and moved on.

Now it was Katie's turn. She reached out over the basket, but her fingers froze, refusing to let go of the applehead.

Drusila whacked Katie's knuckles with a stick. Hard.

Katie didn't dare cry out. Instead she opened her hand. Her mother tumbled into the basket with a sickening *thud.*

26

Katie choked back a sob as she moved ahead with the rest of the zombies. Behind her, Andy dropped their dad into the basket, too.

Katie forced herself to stop thinking about her parents. She couldn't cry. It was too dangerous. She had to figure out what to do next to put her plan into action.

Up ahead, the leader of the line of zombies was heading straight for the barn. Katie could see ghouls waiting there to secure them all with handcuffs and chains. She and Andy had to break free, now!

"Andy," Katie suddenly whispered over her shoulder. "When I say go, run for the bushes."

Katie looked around slowly. It was very dark, and the ghouls were all busy. If she and Andy ran fast enough, maybe no one would notice.

"Go!" she cried, the second she thought the coast was clear.

Andy darted through the bushes like a jackrabbit with his tail on fire.

Katie was right behind him. Together they crouched down in the shrubs.

"I can't believe it!" Andy exclaimed in a whisper. "We made it. No one saw a thing!"

"We have to get to that gift shop," Katie told him.

"There are too many ghouls around," Andy said.

"We'll just have to wait until they chain up all the zombie kids," Katie told her brother. "Maybe then they'll go away."

But that didn't happen. Just moments later, Yaga tore through the parking lot. "Where are those two zombie children?" she screeched at Owen.

Owen put his head down.

"You didn't find them, did you?" Yaga wailed. She shook the scarecrow hard.

Owen moaned, sounding as terrified as Katie felt.

"There's only one hour left!" Yaga screamed. "If I don't have zombie children numbers 458 and 459, my plans will be ruined!"

Drusila scurried over. "There are no children left in town," she informed Yaga. "Every house in Appleton has been searched, and every applehead is accounted for."

"Then those two Lawrence brats must be *here* somewhere," Yaga bellowed. "Find them!"

"Unchain these zombies!" she ordered. "I want every breathing body searching for those two little urchins! And sound the alarms!" she added.

"Uh-oh," Andy gasped as the searchlights snapped on and alarm bells started to ring. "Here we go again!"

"Time is running out!" Yaga shouted.

Katie's stomach churned. That was exactly what she was thinking.

27

As the ghouls and zombies set out to search the property, Katie and Andy plodded zombielike to the gift shop. Time really was running out. They had to move fast.

The door was unlocked, and the shop was empty. Katie was amazed at how easy it was for her and Andy to get inside. It was so easy that for a moment she was afraid it might be some kind of trap.

"Watch outside," Katie told Andy. "Make sure nobody is coming."

Andy kept the door open a tiny crack so that he could peek through it.

Katie headed over to the counter, to where Yaga kept her jar of peanut brittle. She took the lid off the jar, then pulled the squirt bottle of apple cider out of her pocket.

"Here goes," she mumbled.

Carefully, she sprayed the peanut brittle with the cider. She wanted to make sure that she got every piece. But she also had to be careful not to get it too wet. If it was too sticky and gooey, Yaga would know that there was something wrong with it and then she might not eat it.

Give her a taste of her own poison. Martha's words were burned into Katie's brain. *It's the only way to break Yaga's evil spell.*

"I hope this works," Katie said when she was through. She placed the lid back on the jar. "Now let's get out of here," she said to Andy.

"We can't," Andy replied. "Yaga is coming with a bunch of witches and ghouls!"

"What?" Katie started freaking out. But then she realized that the sooner Yaga came into the gift shop, the sooner she would probably eat a piece of peanut brittle. And that was exactly what Katie wanted.

Katie didn't have to tell Andy to hide. He darted behind the boxes in the corner even before she did. Katie barely made it before the door creaked open.

"Somebody had better find those two little brats," Yaga bellowed, "or I promise, you will all pay dearly!"

Yaga was so busy having a fit, Katie was afraid she wouldn't think about eating the peanut brittle.

"Someone will find them," Drusila croaked.

Then Katie heard someone take the lid off the jar of peanut brittle. She knew it was Yaga.

Katie almost giggled. *In just a few short minutes this whole nightmare will be over,* she told herself. And she and Andy would be right there watching when Yaga ate her own poison and turned into an applehead. It was actually a stroke of good luck that she and Andy were trapped inside the gift shop.

Or so Katie thought.

Suddenly, the boxes in front of them crashed to the

ground. It was Drusila who'd kicked them aside. "There they are!" the old hag snarled.

Katie was too startled to scream. She just stared at Yaga, who had been about to bite into a piece of peanut brittle. If one more second had passed before they'd been caught, everything would have been all right, but now it was over.

Katie watched in horror as Yaga threw her peanut brittle onto the floor. "Now you will pay for all the trouble you caused me," the old witch cackled.

28

Drusila grabbed Katie and held her tightly. One of the other witches grabbed Andy.

"Bring them outside," Yaga screamed. Then she stormed out the door.

Katie kicked and screamed as Drusila wrestled her out the door behind Yaga. The other witch dragged Andy outside. He was putting up an even bigger fight than Katie. But it was useless.

We blew it, Katie thought. *We didn't save Mom and Dad or anyone else in Appleton. And now we can't save ourselves.*

According to Martha Grant's diary, everyone in the orchard would disappear at midnight in a burst of fire.

Outside, the sky was pitch black; Katie didn't have to look at her watch to know midnight was just moments away.

"Bring me two apples," Yaga ordered Owen. "Fast!"

Owen scrambled to obey. Quickly, he produced two chunks of apple. Katie shuddered as she saw the worms dangling from them.

Yaga snatched up the apples and stomped over to Andy.

A bunch of ghouls had wrestled Andy to the ground. They held him down so that Yaga could drop the apple chunk into his mouth.

"There's no use trying to fight me," Yaga sneered as she knelt down beside him.

Andy moved his head from side to side to avoid the apple chunk that Yaga pressed against his closed lips. The ghouls held him steady. Yaga held his nose. Still Andy refused to open his mouth.

He held his breath for a long time. But it wasn't long

enough. The instant he parted his lips, gasping for air, Yaga dropped the apple in.

"Hold his mouth shut," she told the ghouls. "Make sure he swallows."

Katie's heart pounded as Yaga turned toward her.

"You hold her for me," she ordered Owen.

Drusila handed Katie over to Owen.

Yaga cackled as she headed toward Katie, holding out the chunk of wormy apple. Katie sealed her lips tightly. Nothing would make her open her mouth.

"Hold her nose," Yaga told Owen.

Katie took one last, deep breath.

But Owen didn't grab her nose. Instead he pushed her aside so hard that she fell to the ground.

"Owen!" Yaga screeched. "Nooooooooo!"

For a second, Katie didn't understand what was going on. Then she looked at Owen. The scarecrow had grabbed Yaga and was holding her tight.

"I-er," Owen bellowed at Katie. "I-er!"

"What?" Katie cried.

Small flames appeared at the hem of Yaga's skirt. It

was midnight. Yaga was starting to burn! In a few more minutes, everyone else would burn, too.

Drusila and the other witches charged at Owen, trying to force him to let go of Yaga. But Owen was bigger and stronger. He managed to keep them at bay and hold on to Yaga at the same time. But there was no telling how long he could keep it up.

"I-er!" Owen yelled impatiently at Katie.

Katie thought he was saying "fire." But then Owen hollered again. "Sssss-i-er!"

Suddenly, Katie understood what Owen wanted. *Ci-der!*

She scrambled to her feet and pulled the bottle of cider out of her pocket. It was still half full.

The flames were licking their way up Yaga's skirt. "I-er!" Owen demanded again. He was having a hard time holding on to the burning witch. But he wasn't giving up.

Katie popped the lid on the bottle as Yaga let out a bloodcurdling scream. Then Katie turned the bottle toward Yaga and squeezed hard, sending a stream of Yaga's own cider into the evil hag's mouth.

That's it! Katie thought triumphantly. *I got her. Now the curse is broken!*

But instead of stopping the fire, Katie's spray of cider only seemed to ignite the blaze. The flames at Yaga's feet exploded, as if they'd been doused with lighter fluid.

Then, in a wild burst of sizzling fire, Yaga disappeared.

29

"Nooooooooo!" Katie cried. "I was too late!" Frantically, she gazed all around, waiting to see the flames engulf everyone else in the orchard.

Andy had spit out the wormy apple and was screaming, too. But it took Katie a full minute to realize what her brother was saying.

"Look! It worked!" he yelled, pointing at Owen's shoes. "Look at Yaga!"

As the smoke started to clear, Katie saw that Yaga had not disappeared at all. She was still there, standing between Owen's enormous black shoes. Only now Yaga was six inches tall, and the ugliest-looking applehead Katie had ever seen.

"We did it!" Katie rejoiced. "We really did it!"

She was so happy, she didn't notice Drusila and the gang of ghouls surrounding her.

"You killed her!" Drusila wailed. "Now you must be killed!" Drusila lunged for Katie's throat. But as she reached out, she herself vanished into thin air.

So did all the rest of the ghouls.

All but Owen, who started to cry.

"You saved my life," he said. "If you two hadn't come along, I—"

"You can talk!" Andy cried, staring at the scarecrow in amazement.

Katie was stunned. Owen *was* speaking, and his voice was gentle and his words were clear.

"Now that Yaga's curse is broken, I can speak," Owen explained. "The moment the evil old hag disappeared, I got back my tongue. Thank you," he added, "for saving my life."

Katie smiled. "No," she told Owen. "You saved *our* lives."

"Why did you help us?" Andy asked.

"Because Yaga was a horrible creature," Owen replied. "And because I didn't want you to be left all alone like my sister," he added sadly.

"Your sister?" Katie repeated. "Who's that?" But suddenly she knew. It was the girl in the diary. That was why Owen had left the diary for them.

"My sister was Martha Grant," Owen explained. "When we were little, our parents brought us here for a hayride, too. And Yaga gave us apples and cider to take on the ride. Just like she gave them to you. Only Martha didn't like apples," Owen went on. "So I ate them both."

Katie thought about her own parents and started to cry, too. "So Yaga turned you into a zombie, and your mom and dad into appleheads," she said sadly.

"Worse," Owen went on. "Yaga was so mad that Martha got away, she decided to take it out on me. She didn't want to leave me a zombie like the rest of the kids, because then I wouldn't remember a thing. So she took out my tongue and gave back my memory. That way, I'd remember every evil thing she had done to my parents and Martha and the rest of the town, but I wouldn't be able to tell a soul. For the past hundred years, I've been Yaga's personal slave."

"So you're like a hundred years old, then, huh?" Andy asked Owen.

"A hundred and ten," Owen answered. "But my heart's still young." He took off his scarecrow mask. His face was more wrinkled than any face Katie had ever seen. But it wasn't scary-looking at all. It was gentle and kind. His black, giant eyes shone with joy.

"Wait a minute." Katie suddenly had a thought. "How come you didn't disappear with all the witches and ghouls?" she asked Owen.

"Because I helped break the curse," he explained. "I've been reading about breaking spells in Yaga's books. That's how I knew what to do."

"What about our mom and dad?" Andy asked. "And everybody else in Appleton?"

Katie had been wondering the same thing.

"It's too late for the kids from hundreds of years ago," Owen answered. "But you've saved everybody who was at the orchard yesterday."

"So where are they?" Katie looked around.

"Just be patient," Owen said. "This spell-breaking takes a few minutes."

Katie looked at Owen, confused.

"Don't worry," he told her. "Everything is going to go back to the way it was before Yaga reappeared. It'll be as if none of this ever happened."

"You mean our parents won't even know they were appleheads?" Andy asked.

"Right," Owen said. "In just a few seconds, it's going to be yesterday again."

"Get out of here." Katie couldn't believe it.

Owen grinned. "Watch," he told them. "Even the sun is going to come back out."

"Yeah, right." Andy couldn't believe it, either.

But Owen was telling the truth. Seconds later, it started to happen. The sun was rising. But it wasn't rising in the east, it was rising in the west. And it was crossing the sky backwards.

The cars that the ghouls had pushed into the lake were rolling out of the water and back to the parking lot.

Even the hands on Katie's watch started spinning backward.

"This is too cool!" Andy exclaimed, watching in amazement.

Katie thought it was pretty cool, too. Especially when the coolest thing of all happened.

"Look!" Katie shrieked, pointing toward the gift shop. "Here come Mom and Dad!"

They were walking out of the gift shop holding hands, acting just as goofy as ever.

30

Mom! Dad!" Katie and Andy exclaimed as they ran for their parents. "You're not appleheads anymore!"

"Excuse me?" Mrs. Lawrence said.

"You're not an applehead!" Katie repeated, hugging her mother.

"Katie," Mr. Lawrence scolded. "What in the world would make you call your mother an applehead?"

"You were an applehead, too, Dad," Andy informed him. "Katie and I saved you!"

"Owen, the scarecrow, helped us," Katie added.

"What are you two talking about?" Mrs. Lawrence asked.

Katie and Andy started from the beginning. They didn't leave out a single detail. But their parents didn't believe a word.

"You guys are too much," Mr. Lawrence chuckled. "You were complaining when we got here," he said. "And now you're making up scary stories about the place."

"We're not making them up!" Andy insisted.

Their parents shot each other amused looks.

"Well, I'm glad you two had such a good time," Mr. Lawrence said. "But I think it's time to go now."

"Home?" Katie asked hopefully.

"No," Mrs. Lawrence answered, looking at her watch. "It's still early enough to catch one last sight."

Katie and Andy groaned. They were exhausted. The last thing they wanted to do was see more historical sights.

"Come on," Mr. Lawrence said, heading for the car. "Let's get a move on it."

"We'll be right there," Katie told him. "As soon as we say good-bye to Owen."

Owen was standing under the giant shade tree holding Yaga in his hands.

"They don't even know they were appleheads," Andy told Owen.

"I told you," Owen said.

Katie looked around the orchard at all the adults who had been appleheads. Now they were surrounded by the kids who had been zombies. They were all laughing and talking like nothing had happened. "They really don't remember anything, do they?" she asked Owen.

"Nope," Owen said. "But we do." He gave them a wink.

"What about her?" Andy asked, pointing to shriveled-up Yaga.

"She's harmless now," Owen said. "This rotten old applehead will never bother anybody ever again."

"What about you?" Katie asked.

Owen shrugged. "I'm not sure," he said. "But I still

have the heart of a young person, so I think I've got some good years left in me. I think I'll stay right here and run the orchard," Owen decided. "The right way. Maybe you two can even come help me once in a while."

Katie smiled. "You bet," she said.

"Yeah," Andy agreed. "That'll be fun."

Just then their father blew the car horn. "Kids!" he called. "Let's go!"

"We'll see you around, Owen," Katie said as she and Andy headed for the car.

"Guess what we're going to see next?" their mother asked a few minutes later.

Mr. Lawrence turned down the bumpiest road Katie had ever been on.

"What?" Katie asked, afraid to hear the answer.

"Appleton Lagoon," their mother informed them. "It sounds pretty neat. Listen to what the guidebook says."

Katie and Andy looked at one another worriedly.

Their mother started to read. "'Legend has it that Appleton Lagoon is home to the biggest sea serpent in the world, even bigger than the Loch Ness Monster.'"

"Who knows?" Mr. Lawrence chuckled. "Maybe we'll spot him."

Katie hoped not.

"Oh, look," her mother said, pointing up ahead. "There it is."

As the car turned onto the road that led to the lagoon, Katie and Andy had to laugh. Appleton Lagoon looked more like a small lake than the home of a giant sea serpent.

"Come on, kids," Mrs. Lawrence said, climbing out of the car. "This is going to be fun."

Katie and Andy followed their parents to the lagoon. Based on what she now knew of Appleton's history, Katie wasn't sure what to expect. But luckily, there wasn't anything to see but a lot of dirty, murky lagoon water.

"Boy, Mom," Katie grumbled. "This was really great."

"Yeah," Andy agreed. "Now let's go home."

Just then their father spotted a nest of birds up in an oak tree. "Oh, look, honey," he said, pointing up. "There's a robins' nest up there."

"Where?" Mrs. Lawrence struggled to see.

"Come around here," Mr. Lawrence said, moving behind the tree. "You'll be able to see better."

Katie and Andy rolled their eyes at each other.

"Terrific," Andy huffed. "Now we're going to be here for hours looking at birds."

But Andy was wrong.

Katie saw the water in the lagoon start to part. Something big rose straight up from the center.

Andy gasped when he saw it, too; an enormous green sea monster with two pointed fangs.

"Uh, Mom?" Katie could barely choke the words out. "We've got a problem here!"

"We'll be with you in just one second, Katie," her mother called from under the oak tree.

"We don't have one second!" Katie cried.

The sea serpent stretched out its long, giant neck. Before Katie could even scream, it opened its mouth, ready to swallow up the oak tree . . . and the two goofy parents standing under it.

Don't miss the next spine-tingling book in the DEADTIME STORIES® series

LITTLE MAGIC SHOP OF HORRORS

1

Peter Newman twisted in his seat, squirming in unbearable pain. He held his hands tightly over his ears. Still, he couldn't escape the bloodcurdling sound.

Peter's best friend, Bo Wilson, tugged on his arm. "What does that sound like to you?" he asked over the hideous wailing.

Peter shrugged helplessly. He couldn't begin to describe the horrible noise.

Bo answered his own question. "It sounds like cats being slaughtered."

That was exactly what it sounded like! Murder. Pure, bloody murder.

Why isn't anybody putting a stop to this? Peter thought. *It's cruel and inhuman to allow this to continue.*

But continue it did.

More than two dozen people, Peter and Bo included, just sat there as Gerald MacDougal worked his instrument of torture.

"Bagpipes," Peter groaned. That was Gerald's evil instrument. "What kind of dweeb plays the bagpipes?" he went on, slumping down in his seat at the back of the school auditorium.

Bo laughed. "He's the worse act yet," he said in Peter's ear.

Peter had to agree. In the half-hour since the

school day had ended, he and Bo had seen some pretty awful acts, but Gerald MacDougal's was definitely the worst.

"The kid's got guts," Peter told Bo. "No talent. But a whole lot of guts."

"Too bad for him this is supposed to be a talent competition." Bo laughed even harder.

It was the auditions for the school talent show. The show was being held at the end of the week, and twelve acts would be chosen. But judging from what he'd seen so far, Peter didn't think it was going to be much of a competition.

Bo was enjoying it, though. He was having a great time making fun of all the kids up onstage. He'd even brought along snacks.

As Gerald gave one last agonizing yowl on the bagpipes, Bo tore into the wrapper of another candy bar. He broke it in two, handing half to Peter. Then he tossed the empty wrapper over his shoulder.

"Don't throw the garbage on the floor," Peter scolded

him. "We'll get into trouble. We're not even supposed to be eating in here."

"Nobody's paying attention to us," Bo said as the teachers sitting in the front row politely applauded Gerald's awful performance. "Who cares about . . ."

"What's this?" A deep voice cut off Bo's words.

Bo was wrong. Somebody *was* paying attention to them.

Peter and Bo froze in their seats, eyes straight ahead. Neither of them had the courage to turn around and face the voice.

The discarded candy wrapper dropped from above into Bo's lap. Still, neither Peter nor Bo moved.

"No eating in the auditorium," the voice said.

Peter glanced over his shoulder. The school janitor loomed over them.

Janitor Bob was more than six feet tall and was built like a professional football player. But for someone so big, he moved as silently as a shadow. He was always appearing out of nowhere to catch kids doing what they shouldn't be doing. This time he'd caught the two of them.

"That's strike two," Janitor Bob said, holding up two enormous gloved fingers.

"Strike two?" Bo repeated, practically jumping out of his seat. "How can that be strike two?" he protested. "We don't even have a strike one."

"Oh, really?" Janitor Bob glared down at them. "Who drew the lovely picture of Mrs. Dingleman on the mirror in the boys' room last week?"

Mrs. Dingleman was the principal. And the picture in the boys' room wasn't "lovely" at all. It was actually pretty rude.

Peter and Bo exchanged guilty looks. But neither said a word.

"One more strike and you're out," Janitor Bob whispered menacingly. Then he turned around and headed through the back doors of the auditorium as silently as he'd entered.

"Oh, man," Bo sighed. "No way Psycho Bob knows we drew that picture."

"Yes, way!" Peter shot back. "Didn't you hear what he said?"

Every kid in school was scared of Janitor Bob. Because every kid in the school knew that he had superhuman strength and a superexplosive temper. Peter had heard that Janitor Bob once lifted an entire school bus by himself, just to move it out of his parking spot. Even if the story wasn't true, Janitor Bob was not somebody Peter wanted to mess with.

"What do you suppose happens when you get three strikes?" Peter asked nervously.

"I don't know," Bo answered. "Nobody's ever gotten three strikes before. At least nobody who's lived to tell about it. For all I know, he may just kill you and bury you in that basement office of his."

"Don't drop any more wrappers," Peter ordered Bo. "There's no way I want to get three strikes."

"Okay, okay," Bo said. "Now shut up. We're missing the whole show."

The next act was almost over. It was two girls from Peter's class dancing around the stage in frilly tutus.

They looked pretty silly. But they'd finished their dance before Peter and Bo could start making fun of them.

"Look who's up next." Bo nudged Peter with his elbow.

"Oh, puke!" Peter groaned. "It's Mary-Margaret Mahoney." He spit out the name like he was spitting out poison. "I hate that girl."

"Me, too," Bo said. "She thinks she's such hot stuff."

The two of them cringed as Mary-Margaret Mahoney strutted onto the stage in a bright red, rhinestone-studded cowgirl costume, carrying a baton.

"Oh, brother," Peter said. "She's going to twirl her stupid baton again."

"Of course she is," Bo told him. "It's the only talent she's got."

Peter laughed. "So what's she going to be when she grows up—a professional baton twirler?"

"No," Bo answered. "She's going to be Miss America. Remember? That's what she always tells everybody."

"Not with that face, she isn't," Peter said. "I'd be surprised if she could win a dog show."

"For real," Bo agreed. "But she's been bragging all week about how she's going to win the school talent show. She just might do it, too. It's not like she has any competition. Besides, she really does know how to twirl that baton. She's even won state competitions."

"I know, I know." Peter rolled his eyes. "Every time she gets her stupid picture in the paper, Mrs. Dingleman puts it up on the bulletin board. Then Mary-Margaret walks around like she really *is* Miss America. If she wins this show, she'll be totally obnoxious about it."

"Well, she's going to win," Bo said. "Look." He pointed toward the stage.

Mary-Margaret was standing at the foot of the stage. She handed her baton to her mother, who'd been whispering something to the teachers who were judging. Peter watched as Mrs. Dingleman, the head judge, nodded at Mrs. Mahoney.

A second later, Mrs. Mahoney lit the baton on fire and handed it back to Mary-Margaret.

"A fire baton!" Peter was shocked. "I can't believe they're letting her do a fire baton in school."

"They let Mary-Margaret do anything she wants to do," Bo griped. "Besides, it's the fire baton that always wins her the state competitions. The teachers think it's great."

"If Mary-Margaret gets to dance around with fire, she's sure to win," Peter moaned.

Bo grinned. "Not if we do something to mess her up."

"Like what?" Peter asked.

Bo didn't answer. He was too busy fishing around inside his backpack. A second later, he pulled out a rubber band and a bag of peanut M&Ms.

Mary-Margaret's hoe-down music started to play. Within seconds, her silver baton was a fiery blur. She passed it behind her back and under her leg. Then she tossed it high up into the air and caught it.

With every trick, the judges burst into loud applause. Mary-Margaret danced around the stage, smiling smugly.

But not for long.

Bo loaded a peanut M&M into the slingshot he'd created with the rubber band and his fingers. He took careful aim and let it rip.

A second later, catastrophe struck. But as Peter watched, it felt as if it were happening in slow motion.

Mary-Margaret had turned sideways. She'd lifted her leg to pass her fire baton beneath it. Suddenly, the peanut M&M hit her in the butt, and Mary-Margaret let out a loud squeal. The fire baton flew into the air, twirling out of control.

Peter started to laugh. He thought it was the funniest thing he'd ever seen—until the swirling ball of flames slammed right into the stage curtains.

ABOUT THE AUTHORS

As sisters, Annette and Gina Cascone share the same last name. As writers, they sometimes share the same brain. As children, they found it difficult to share anything at all.

The Cascone sisters grew up in Lawrenceville, New Jersey. It was there that Annette and Gina began making up stories. Since their father was a criminal attorney, and their mother claimed to have ESP, the Cascone sisters honed their storytelling skills early on in life—mainly to stay out of trouble. These days, they're telling their crazy stories to anyone who will listen.

Here are the stats: Gina is older; Annette is not. Gina is married; Annette should be. Gina has two children; Annette borrowed one. Gina has a granddaughter; Annette has a grandniece. Gina has cats; Annette has dogs. They both have a sister named Elise.

Visit Annette and Gina at www.agcascone.com.